Florence Holbrook

Dramatic Reader

Florence Holbrook

Dramatic Reader

1st Edition | ISBN: 978-3-75237-470-4

Place of Publication: Frankfurt am Main, Germany

Year of Publication: 2020

Outlook Verlag GmbH, Germany.

DRAMATIC READER
BY

FLORENCE HOLBROOK

LITTLE RED RIDING-HOOD

PERSONS IN THE PLAY—LITTLE RED RIDING-HOOD, MOTHER, BIRD, WOLF, MILLER, GRANDMOTHER

SCENE I.—*At Red Riding-Hood's Home*

Mother. Would you like to go to grandmother's to-day, my child? The sun is bright and the air is warm and pleasant.

Little Red Riding-Hood. Yes, mother, you know I always like to visit dear grandmamma.

Mother. Then you may go. You may carry your little basket, and I'll put some honey and a jar of butter in it for grandma.

Little Red Riding-Hood. Oh, that will be a nice present for her! And may I take her some flowers?

Mother. Yes, dear child. Gather some of those you like best.

Little Red Riding-Hood. Here they are, mother—roses and pansies! Aren't they pretty?

Mother. Very pretty and sweet. Now put on your little red cloak and take the basket. Be very careful as you pass through the wood, and go directly to grandma's house.

Little Red Riding-Hood. Yes, dear mother. Nothing will harm me. All the birds and animals love me and I love them.

Mother. Good-by, little daughter. Give me a kiss and take my love to dear grandmother.

Little Red Riding-Hood. Good-by, mamma: good-by!

SCENE II.—*In the Wood*

Little Red Riding-Hood (singing).

Good morning, merry sunshine,
How did you come so soon?
You chase the little stars away
And shine away the moon.
I saw you go to sleep last night

Before I ceased my playing.
How did you get 'way over there,
And where have you been staying?

How pretty it is here in the wood! Oh, what a lovely bed of moss! You must come with me, pretty green moss, to grandma's house. Good morning, pretty bird: will you sing to me this morning?

Bird. Yes, little Red Riding-Hood. I will sing to you because you love all the birds and can understand my song. Soon I'll show you my little birds who are just big enough to fly.

Little Red Riding-Hood. Thank you, dear bird, I shall be glad to see the cunning little things. But now I must hurry to grandmother's with the butter and the honey. Good-by!

Bird. Good-by, little friend! Chirp, chirp; chirp, chirp!

Little Red Riding-Hood. Now the little bird has flown away. I must put this moss in my basket and then hurry along—

Wolf. Ugh, ugh!

Little Red Riding-Hood. Oh! how you frightened me, Mister Wolf! Where did you come from?

Wolf. From my pretty cave, far, far in the dark wood, little girl. What is your name?

Little Red Riding-Hood. Why, don't you know me? I'm little Red Riding-Hood.

Wolf. I'm a stranger in this place, little girl; but I shall know you the next time I see you—ugh, ugh! What have you in your pretty basket, little Red Riding-Hood? It smells like honey.

Little Red Riding-Hood. It *is* honey, Mr. Wolf. I am taking it to my dear grandmother.

Wolf. Are you all alone in the wood, my child? Isn't your mother with you? Aren't you afraid?

Little Red Riding-Hood. Afraid? no, indeed! Why should I be afraid? All the animals are my friends.

Wolf. Oh, yes, of course they are all your friends! But is it far to your grandmother's house?

Little Red Riding-Hood. No, Mr. Wolf, only about half a mile. You go down this path to the mill and then turn to the right, and the first house you come to is my grandmother's. It's a little red house.

Wolf. Oh, that is very easy to find! But I know a shorter way through the wood. Let us run a race and see who will get there first.

Little Red Riding-Hood. All right, Mr. Wolf. Good-by!

Wolf. Ugh, ugh; good-by!

Little Red Riding-Hood. How fast he runs! I know he will win the race. How surprised dear grandma will be when Mr. Wolf knocks at the door! Now I see the mill. I will sing the pretty mill song we learned in school the other day.

[*Begins to sing, then stops suddenly.*]

Oh, there is the miller. Good morning, Mr. Miller! Have you seen Mr. Wolf go by?

Miller. No, little Red Riding-Hood. Have you seen a wolf in the wood?

Little Red Riding-Hood. Yes, Mr. Miller, and he said he would race with me to my grandmother's house.

Miller. My dear child, I will call the men who are chopping trees in the forest and they will catch Mr. Wolf. He is no friend of ours, and you must not talk with him, for he is cruel and will do you harm.

Little Red Riding-Hood. Will he? Then I will never say another word to him. But I must hurry on to dear grandmother's.

SCENE III.—*Grandmother's House*

Little Red Riding-Hood. Here I am at the door; I will knock. May I come in, dear grandmother?

Wolf (in the house). Open the latch and walk in.

Little Red Riding-Hood. Here I am, dear grandmother! I am so glad the bad wolf did not get here first. Are you so sick you must stay in bed? See the nice butter and honey that mother sent you. And see the pretty flowers I've brought you.

Wolf. Thank you, my child.

Little Red Riding-Hood. How rough your voice is, grandmother!

Wolf. That's because I've such a bad cold.

Little Red Riding-Hood. But how bright your eyes are, grandmother!

Wolf. The better to see you, my child.

Little Red Riding-Hood. How long your arms are, grandmother!

Wolf. The better to hold you, my child.

Little Red Riding-Hood. And how big your teeth are, grandmother!

Wolf. The better to eat you—ugh! ugh!

[*The miller and the wood choppers rush in.*]

Mr. Miller. Here's an end to you, Mr. Wolf! These men with their axes will stop your cruel deeds.

[*The wolf runs out, followed by the men.*]

Come, little Red Riding-Hood, don't be afraid. The wolf can't harm you now. Here is your grandmother, who has just come home from the village. She will take care of you.

Little Red Riding-Hood. Dear grandmother! I thought that the wolf was you.

Grandmother. Darling little Red Riding-Hood! How glad I am that you are safe. Now you must stay with me till your mother comes, and we will tell her how the brave men saved you and me from the hungry wolf. Won't she be glad to see her little Red Riding-Hood again?

GOLDILOCKS, OR THE THREE BEARS

PERSONS IN THE PLAY—GOLDILOCKS, THE DOLLIE, FATHER BEAR, MOTHER BEAR, BABY BEAR

SCENE I.—*Goldilocks in the Garden with her Doll*

Goldilocks. O dear! I do wish mother would come home. I am going to meet her. She told me not to go out of the garden lest I should get lost; but if I keep in the road, I *can't* get lost! Come, Dollie, you and I will go just a little way to meet mamma.

How warm it is in the sunshine! I think we shall go into the shady wood a little while. Let us pick some of these pretty flowers to make a wreath—won't mother be surprised when I show her all these flowers. Here is a lovely red one; and here's another like a daisy.

How dark it is here! I cannot see the road. I wonder if I'm lost! O mamma, mamma! I'm afraid. Dear Dollie, I'm glad you are with me.

Dollie. But I'm afraid, too!

Goldilocks. Please, dear Dollie, don't be afraid. Why, there's nothing to be afraid of—oh!

Dollie. What is the matter, Goldilocks?

Goldilocks. Look, what is that?

Dollie. I don't see anything.

Goldilocks. I thought I saw a bear.

Dollie. Well, I hope not. I don't like bears.

Goldilocks. But there is a little house. Isn't it a funny little house? I wonder who lives there!

Dollie. Dear Goldilocks, please, don't you think we'd better go home? I don't like strange little houses in the wood.

Goldilocks. Perhaps a kind fairy lives there who will show us the way home.

Dollie. Yes, or perhaps she is the Gingerbread Witch who will turn us into gingerbread for her supper!

Goldilocks. Don't say such uncomfortable things, Dollie. She couldn't turn you into gingerbread, anyway.

7

Dollie. Well, I know I'm made of sawdust, but she might make mush of me for breakfast!

Goldilocks. I know you're fooling now, dear Dollie. Let's look in the window. I don't see anyone. I'll knock at the door. No one answers. Come, Dollie, we'll open the door and walk in. How nice and warm it is. There is a good fire in the kitchen stove.

Dollie. Yes, and I smell something good to eat.

Goldilocks. Here it is on the table—what pretty bowls—one, two, three! I'll taste the porridge in the big bowl first. O Dollie, it is too hot! I burned my mouth.

Dollie. Try the next bowl. Perhaps the porridge in the middle-sized bowl is not so hot.

Goldilocks. No, indeed, it isn't; but it is too cold.

Dollie. Aren't you hard to please? I'm so hungry I could eat anything.

Goldilocks. Now this in the little bowl is just right. Sit down, Dollie, and we'll eat it all up.

Dollie. Do you think it is very polite for us to eat it all?

Goldilocks. You should have spoken of that before. It is too late now when it is all gone. Come, let us go into the parlor.

Dollie. Don't you think we'd better go home?

Goldilocks. How can we when I don't know the way? I'm tired, and I think I'll rest awhile in this nice big rocking-chair. But it's too high; I can't get into it.

Dollie. Don't move it out of its place.

Goldilocks. Never mind! I'll try the middle-sized chair. I don't like this, it is too low.

Dollie. Well, Goldilocks, you must not put chairs out of their places!

Goldilocks. Oh, it won't hurt them. Now let us try this pretty little chair. Come, Dollie, I'll sing you a song:

> Rock-a-bye,
> Dollie,
> in
> the
> treetop,

9

When the
wind
blows,
the
cradle
will
rock;
When the
bough
breaks,
the
cradle
will
fall
And down
will
come
Dollie,
cradle
and
all!

[*Chair breaks.*]

Dollie. Well, something broke then!

Goldilocks. Yes, the cradle and all came down that time. Dear, O dear! I wish I hadn't rocked you so hard. I wish I hadn't run away! [*Crying.*]

Dollie. Don't cry, dear Goldilocks. Let us see what we can find in the next room. Perhaps some one is in there who will take us to your dear mother.

Goldilocks. O Dollie! I'm a naughty girl not to mind my mother. If I'd only stayed at home in the garden!

Dollie. Oh, see the big bed!

Goldilocks. I'm so tired I believe I'll climb in and go to sleep. But I don't like it. This big bed is too hard.

Dollie. And this middle-sized one is too soft.

Goldilocks. But this little one is *just right.* Go—to—sleep—Dollie—

SCENE II.—*The Bear Family in the Wood*

Father Bear. Well, little son, aren't you about ready to go home?

Sonny Bear. Oh, no, father! Let me play just a little longer. Here are such good places to hide in the shady wood.

Mother Bear. No, dear little sonny, we must go home now. It is getting late. It's time for you to have your supper and go to bed.

Sonny Bear. All right, mother dear. I believe I am hungry, and your porridge is always so good.

Mother Bear. Most children like porridge. Perhaps you can have a nice red apple, too.

Sonny Bear. Oh, goody! Little sonny bears always like apples, don't they, papa?

Father Bear. Yes, my dear. Mother, let me take your knitting basket. What are you making now?

Mother Bear. A warm cap for sonny. Isn't it pretty?

Father Bear. Very pretty, and he should be very glad he has such a good mother.

Sonny Bear. She *is* a good mother, and you are a very good father, too.

Father Bear. Well, here we are at home again. But the door is open. I'm certain I closed it when we went away. Who has been here?

Mother Bear. Let us take off our wraps and have our tea.

Father Bear. Why, somebody has been tasting my porridge.

Mother Bear. What? Let me see! Some one has left a spoon in my porridge, too.

Sonny Bear. Oh, mamma! Look at my bowl! Some one has eaten my porridge all up.

Mother Bear. Never mind, sonny boy, you may have some of mine. But I wonder who has been here. Let us go into the parlor and see if anyone is there.

Father Bear. Who's been moving my chair?

Mother Bear. Some one has been sitting in my chair!

Sonny Bear. Look, mother! Some one has been rocking in my chair and broken it all to pieces! O dear! my nice little chair!

Father Bear. Never mind, Sonny Bear; don't cry. I'll buy you another chair at Mr. Wolf's store to-morrow.

Mother Bear. And now it is time for us to go to bed. Our little son is tired and sleepy.

Father Bear. I'll carry him up stairs. Come, sonny, there you are up on my shoulder.

> Ride a cock horse to Banbury Cross
> To see an old woman ride on a white horse.
> With rings on her fingers and bells on her toes,
> She shall have music wherever she goes!

Well, who's been in my bed, I'd like to know?

Mother Bear. Why, look at my bed. Some one has been lying on my bed!

Sonny Bear. Come quick, Mother! Father, come! Some one is in my bed.

Goldilocks (*waking and frightened*). Oh, see the three Bears. Come, Dollie, let us jump out of the window. [*Runs away.*]

Mother Bear. The little girl has gone, dear. Now you must go to sleep.

THE BIRD WITH THE BROKEN WING

PERSONS IN THE PLAY—The Bird, The Oak Tree, The Maple, The Willow, The Spruce, The Pine, The Juniper, The Forest Fairy, Jack Frost

Scene I.—*In the Woods*

The Oak. See that flock of birds coming! The winter is near and they are flying south.

The Maple. I hope they will not light on my branches; I like to keep my leaves in order.

The Willow. So many birds will break my tender twigs. I am sure I do not want them either. Here they come!

[*The birds fly over the trees.*]

Little Bird. Oh, I can fly no farther! My wing is broken and I cannot hold it up. I am so tired and cold and hungry! I must rest to-night in this forest. I am sure some big strong tree will give me a resting place. I will ask this tall Oak, he looks so strong and his leaves are so thick and warm! May I rest in your branches to-night, great Oak Tree? I am a poor little bird with a broken wing and I am cold and tired and hungry.

The Oak. I am sorry; but my branches are all engaged by the squirrels, who are getting their acorns in for the winter. I have no room for strange birds.

Little Bird. Oh! I am so lonely, so tired! Surely the handsome Maple Tree will take me in. She has no acorns and so the squirrels will not be in her branches. Kind, lovely Maple Tree, may I rest to-night in your branches? I am a poor little bird with a broken wing. I will not harm your pretty leaves.

The Maple. My leaves tremble to think of taking in strange birds! My house is in perfect order and I cannot think of disturbing it. Please go away!

Little Bird. Oh, what shall I do? The Oak and the Maple are so unkind and I am shivering with cold and weak with hunger. Surely *some* tree must be kind. Dear Willow, you are kind, are you not? Will you take me upon your graceful branches just for to-night?

The Willow. Really, Mr. Bird with the broken wing, I think you should have gone on with the other birds. I cannot take you in. I do not know your name or anything about you. Besides, I am very sleepy, and so, good night!

Little Bird. Oh, my dear bird friends, how I wish some of you were here! I shall perish with the cold if I must stay on the ground. Where can I go? The Oak, the Maple, and the Willow have all turned me away and the night is coming on.

The Spruce. Dear little bird with the broken wing, come to me! Can you hop up into my branches if I hold them down to you? See, here I am! I am not so handsome as the Maple tree, but my leaves grow thick and I'll try to keep you warm through the night. Come!

Little Bird. Dear Spruce tree, how kind you are! I did not see you at first. Yes, here I am, on your lowest branch. How cosy and warm I feel. Oh, you are so good, and I was so tired and cold. Here I'll rest. I wish I could ever thank you enough for your goodness.

The Spruce. Do not speak of that, dear little bird; I am ashamed of the proud, selfish trees that would not shelter you. Should we not all be kind and helpful to one another?

The Pine. Well said, sister Spruce. And I will do my best to help you. I am not so strong as the Oak tree, little bird, but I will stand between you and the cold north wind. Rest warm and safe in the branches of the kind Spruce tree.

Little Bird. I thank you, tall Pine tree, for your kindness. You are a good brother of the Spruce and I shall rest well while you are both taking care of me.

The Juniper. I cannot keep the strong north wind from you, little bird with the broken wing, but if you are hungry, you may eat of my berries. Perhaps then you will rest better.

Little Bird. Thank you, dear Juniper tree. Why are you all so kind to me? Your berries are good, and now I am cold and hungry no longer. I'll go to sleep.

Good night, dear trees!

Trees. Good night, little bird, and may you have sweet dreams!

SCENE II.—*Midnight in the Forest*

Jack Frost. Here I am in the great forest. How I dislike to touch all these beautiful leaves; yet I must obey the orders of King Winter. Here comes the Forest Fairy. Do you know why I have come, dear Fairy of the Forest?

Forest Fairy. Yes, Mr. Frost. I know that you must touch all the leaves, turning them into brilliant hues of gold and crimson and brown. I dislike to have them go, and yet you and I must obey the commands of King Winter. But,—

Jack Frost. But what, dear Fairy? You speak as if you had some wish to make —what is it?

Forest Fairy. I must tell you. Such a dear little bird came to the forest this evening. He had a broken wing, and he was cold and very tired. He asked shelter from the great Oak, the proud Maple, and the graceful Willow,—and all refused. I was so ashamed of my trees!

Jack Frost. What! did all the trees refuse to help a poor, tired little bird?

Forest Fairy. Listen! just as I was intending to speak to the trees, I heard the Spruce tell him to come to her branches and she would give him shelter. Then the Pine tree offered to keep the north wind from him, and the Juniper gave him her berries to eat. Could you, dear Jack Frost—

Jack Frost. Yes, yes, I know what you would ask. Such kindness as this should meet with some reward. The leaves of the proud Oak, the Maple, and the Willow shall fall to the ground when the cold of winter comes; but the Spruce, the Pine, the Juniper, and all their family shall keep their leaves and they shall be green all through the year. They shall be called the Evergreen Trees.

CORNELIA AND HER JEWELS

PERSONS IN THE PLAY—CORNELIA, NYDIA THE MAID, JULIA, ELDER SON, YOUNGER SON

SCENE.—*Home of Cornelia*

Nydia. Madam, the lady Julia waits to salute you.

Cornelia. Bid her enter, I pray. It is not fitting to have her wait.

Nydia. She is at the door, gracious madam.

Cornelia. Welcome, thrice welcome, fair Julia.

[*Nydia carries Julia's casket.*]

Julia. Thanks, dear Cornelia, for your kind greeting. May you and all your household have peace and joy.

Cornelia. And may those blessings be yours also, dear Julia. But tell me, what treasures have you in that charming casket?

Julia. A few poor jewels, fair friend. Bring me the casket, Nydia. These are some presents my parents and husband have given me.

Cornelia. I am so glad you have brought them to show me. You are very kind, for you know I greatly admire beautiful jewels.

Julia. See, here is a pearl necklace.

Cornelia. How lovely! Let me clasp it about your neck. It is very becoming. And what other gems have you?

Julia. Here is a girdle my mother gave me for a wedding present. Isn't it pretty?

Cornelia. Pretty! my dear, it is exquisite! Your mother showed much good taste when she chose this for you.

Julia. And here are some rings from the far East. See these emeralds and rubies; how they flash in the sunlight!

Cornelia. How well they look on your white hands! But I see something else.

Julia. Yes, this is my handsomest jewel, a diamond bracelet. This I like best of all.

Cornelia. They are all lovely, my dear friend, and I am glad you have such

17

beautiful things.

Julia. But, dear Cornelia, where are your jewels? All Rome knows how rich your famous father, Scipio, was, and surely he gave you many handsome ornaments. Please show them to me.

Cornelia. Oh, no, dear friend. But hark! I think I hear my sons. Nydia, tell them I wish to see them.

Nydia. Here are the children, madam.

The Boys (*running in*). Dear mother! darling mother!

Cornelia. Tell me, my Caius, what did the pedagogue teach you to-day?

Caius. O mother! It was wonderful! He told us how Horatius kept the bridge in the brave days of old. Wasn't that a great and noble deed, mother mine?

Cornelia. Yes, my darling. And you, my Tiberius, have you been pleased with your lessons?

Cornelia and her Jewels

Tiberius. Mother, how you must honor our grandfather, the noble Scipio! Our teacher told the boys of his great campaigns in Africa and how the Senate called him Africanus after the war was over.

Cornelia. Yes, my son, such work and such lives are lessons worthy of study. They teach the young how they too may live and die for their beloved country.

Caius. I shall try to be a brave man some day, too, dear mother.

Tiberius. And I, mother, shall try to be worthy of our noble family.

Cornelia. My dear, noble boys! Julia, these are my jewels.

Julia. How you shame my vanity, noble Cornelia! What are all the precious stones in the world compared with these noble boys! Daughter of the famous Scipio, the world will remember you through the great deeds of your sons, and all mankind will honor you as CORNELIA, MOTHER OF THE GRACCHI.

CINDERELLA

PERSONS IN THE PLAY—CINDERELLA, MOTHER, FATHER, KATHERINE, ELIZABETH, FAIRY GODMOTHER, PRINCE, HERALD

SCENE I.—*Cinderella's Home*

Mother. I am so glad we are all invited to the ball at the Prince's palace. You know, my dear, that it will be a great pleasure for our girls.

Father. Yes; and I suppose you will all have to buy new ball dresses.

Katherine. O mamma! isn't it lovely! May I have a blue silk dress?

Elizabeth. And may I have pink, dear mother? And shall we get them to-day?

Mother. Yes, my child; and you may both go with me to buy your dresses and slippers.

Cinderella. Dear papa, may I go to the ball at the Prince's palace?

Father. You, my child! Aren't you too young for parties? Ask your mother.

Cinderella. May I go to the ball, mother?

Mother. Nonsense, child! what are you thinking of? A ball is no place for a child like you. You are better off at home by the kitchen fire.

Cinderella. But I'm fourteen. Sister Katherine, won't you coax mamma to let me go?

Katherine. No, indeed, I'll not! What would you do at a ball? a silly thing like you!

Elizabeth. Don't be a goose. Wait till you're older and better looking. There's no room in the carriage for you, and you are too young, anyway.

Mother. Come, girls, it is time for us to go down town to buy our new gowns. Cinderella, go to your lessons. Don't think any more about the ball. You can't go, and so that's the end of it.

SCENE II.—*Cinderella's Home*

Father. Come, girls! aren't you ready yet? Is your mother coming?

Katherine. Yes, father, in just a minute.

Mother. Here we are, dear. Don't the girls look sweet?

Father. Yes, yes! but, come on, for we are late now.

Mother. Good night, Cinderella. Be a good girl and go to bed at nine o'clock.

[*All go out, leaving Cinderella alone.*]

Cinderella. Good-by!—Now they have gone and I am all alone. Oh, why couldn't I go, too! How pretty they all looked! I would not take up much room, and I don't like to be left here by myself when they are having such a good time. Oh, dear! I believe I'm going to cry, but I can't help it. [*Cries.*]

[*Enter fairy godmother.*]

Fairy Godmother. Why are you crying, Cinderella?

Cinderella. Who is that? I thought I heard some one speaking to me, but I can't see anybody.

Fairy Godmother. What is the matter, Cinderella?

Cinderella. Oh, *lovely* lady! who are you?

Fairy Godmother. I am your fairy godmother, my child, and I wish to know why you are crying.

Cinderella. Oh, dear! I'm crying because they have all gone to the ball; and I wanted to go, too, and they wouldn't take me!

Fairy Godmother. Never mind, my dear. Stop crying, and I will let you go.

Cinderella. Oh, dear fairy godmamma! will you, really? But how *can* I go in this old dress?

Fairy Godmother. You'll see. Tell me, Cinderella, have you a big yellow pumpkin in the kitchen garden?

Cinderella. Yes, I think so. I saw one there yesterday.

Fairy Godmother. Go, get it for me.

Cinderella (*runs out, and returns with the pumpkin*). I've found it! Here it is!

Fairy Godmother. Yes, that is a fine pumpkin. I'll touch it with my wand. What is it now?

[*The pumpkin is changed to a carriage.*]

Cinderella. Oh! oh! how lovely! Such a beautiful, big, yellow coach! Why, it is much finer than papa's black carriage.

Fairy Godmother. I am glad you like your coach. Now do you think there are any rats in your rat trap?

Cinderella. I'll go see. Yes, here is the trap with two big rats in it. What long tails they have!

Fairy Godmother. Wait till I touch them with my fairy wand. Now what do you see?

Cinderella. Oh, dear godmother! what a wonderful wand to change rats into great handsome horses with long manes and tails! You dear horses! I'll get you some sugar to eat.

Fairy Godmother. Don't stop to pet them now, but fetch me the mousetrap.

Cinderella. Here it is with two cunning little mice in it. What will you do with them?

Fairy Godmother. Touch them with my fairy wand and turn them into a coachman and a footman. See, the coachman is on the box with the reins in his hand, and the footman holds the door open for you. Will you step in,

Cinderella?

Cinderella. In *these* clothes, dear godmother?

Fairy Godmother (laughing). That wouldn't be nice, would it? Well, let us see what my wand can do for you. Now look in the glass and tell me what you see there.

Cinderella. Oh, what a pretty lady! Why, I do believe she is myself! What a beautiful dress! And look, dear godmother! see my pretty glass slippers!

Fairy Godmother. Yes, my dear, you are all ready for the Prince's ball. I want you to have a happy time, but remember this. You must start for home when the clock strikes twelve or your pretty clothes will change, your coach will turn into a pumpkin, your horses to rats, and you will have to walk home.

Cinderella. I'll remember, dear godmother, and run away on the first stroke. Thank you so much! Good-by!

[*Enters the coach and is driven away.*]

Scene III.—*The Prince's Palace*

Cinderella. Here I am at the palace. Please announce me as the Lady from Far Away.

Herald. The Lady from Far Away!

Prince. What a lovely lady! she must be a princess. Tell me, fair lady, are you a princess from the land of flowers?

Cinderella. I am not a princess, sir, but only a girl from the land of happy thoughts.

Prince. You say well, fair lady, for no one can look upon you without thoughts of love and joy.

Cinderella. And you, great Prince, have thoughts of great and noble deeds, have you not?

Prince. Yes, I have thoughts of great deeds, of brave men and fair ladies, of games and victories,—but now I have forgotten all but you.

Cinderella. Will you remember me to-morrow or shall I fade away like the dreams of night?

Prince. No dreams could be fairer, but I hope you will not vanish as they do. If you do, I am quite sure that I shall find you!

Cinderella. Don't be too sure, for I am not what I seem. I am a princess only in your thoughts; really I am—

Prince. What? a flower, a star, a goddess?

Cinderella. No, only a woman—

Prince. The best of all, a woman! And now will the dream-woman dance with me?

Cinderella. With pleasure; what lovely music!—and so many pretty women. What beautiful rooms!

[*Cinderella, the Prince, her father, mother, sisters, and two gentlemen dance the minuet.*]

Prince. Will you not tell me your name and where you live?

Cinderella. Both are a secret.

Prince. It makes no difference to me, for I know you, and that is enough.

Cinderella. I hear the clock! What hour is it striking?

Prince. Twelve—but that is early. You need not go?

Cinderella. Yes, I must, and quietly. Do not try to keep me, Prince—good night!

Prince. She is gone! and I do not know where she lives. How can I find her? I'll give another ball and hope she will come again.

[*All go out.*]

Scene IV.—*Cinderella's Home*

Father. Well, girlies, did you have a pleasant time at the ball?

Katherine. Oh, yes, papa, splendid! But did you see the lovely princess that came so late?

Elizabeth. She was the prettiest girl there. I wonder who she is!

Mother. So do I. It seems to me I've seen her somewhere. Perhaps I've met her in my travels; but I can't remember where it was.

Father. What is her name?

Katherine. I heard some one say she was Lady Far Away. But that's not a real name.

Elizabeth. Perhaps she is a princess in disguise.

Cinderella. Tell me, sister, how this princess looked.

Elizabeth. Oh! she is lovely! Golden curls and blue eyes and such a sweet smile!

Katherine. She wore a beautiful dress that shone like the moonlight.

Elizabeth. Did you notice her pretty slippers? They looked like crystal.

Mother. The Prince danced with her all the time.

Father. Why, here comes the Prince's herald. I'll see what he wants. Here is a note. It is an invitation to go to the Prince's palace again to-night. Do you all want to go?

All. Yes, yes, father, please!

Father. All right, we'll go!

Cinderella. Can't I go this time, mamma?

Mother. No, my dear. When you are a little older you can go, but not now.

Scene V.—*At the Palace*

Prince. I wonder if my fairy princess will come to-night. I've been looking for her for more than an hour. Oh, here she is! Dear lady, I've been hoping you would come.

Cinderella. So you have not forgotten me?

Prince. No, and never shall. Will you go with me to see the flowers?

Cinderella. What lovely flowers! This is certainly the home of the flower fairies. See the roses nodding at us. They almost ask us to love them.

Prince. May I give you this dainty pink one? It is the color of your cheeks.

Cinderella. Remember I am from the land of Far Away and I must vanish at midnight.

Prince. Tell me where your father lives that I may call upon him.

Cinderella. Not now; but sometime I may tell you about my fairy godmother.

Prince. There! I knew you must be a sister of the fairies. Does your fairy godmother have a fairy wand?

Cinderella. Yes, and she does wonderful things with it—but my father and mother do not know about her.

Prince. Of course not. Only very young people know about fairy godmothers. But we know, don't we?

Cinderella. Hark! I hear the chimes ringing. It must be twelve o'clock, and I must go.

Prince. Do not go, dear princess. Stay here in my palace, always.

Cinderella. The fairies are calling me and I am late. I must go. Perhaps I can come again sometime. Oh, I am afraid—

Prince. Afraid of what?

Cinderella. Good-by, good-by!

Prince. She's gone! What was she afraid of? I cannot see her! Who is that child running down the stairway? She must be one of the servants who has been watching the dancers. I wish I could see my princess. What is that shining thing on the stairs? She has lost one of her crystal slippers. Now I know how I shall find her. To-morrow I shall send a herald through the city to find the owner of this pretty little slipper.

SCENE VI.—*Cinderella's Home*

Cinderella. Mamma, mamma, here is a man on horseback who wants to see you.

Mother. What is your errand, sir?

Herald. I am sent by the great Prince of our country to find the owner of this slipper. He says he will marry no one but the lady who can wear this little crystal slipper.

Mother. I'll call my daughters. Katherine! Elizabeth! We were all at the ball at the Prince's palace. Katherine, is this your glass slipper? Try it on.

Katherine. Yes, mother. My, how small it is! I cannot get my foot in it!

Elizabeth. Perhaps it will fit me. My feet are smaller than yours. No, I cannot push my foot in, no matter how long I try. It must be a magic slipper.

Cinderella. May I try on the slipper?

Mother. My dear child, why should you try on the slipper? It belongs to the princess who went to the ball.

Katherine. And you were not at the ball, Cinderella!

Elizabeth. Your foot is too big for it, my dear little sister.

Herald. Pardon me, ladies, but the orders of the Prince are that every lady, young or old, must try on the slipper, and when the owner is found she must go with me to the palace.

Cinderella. Give it to me, please. See how easily it slips on my foot—and here is the mate to the glass slipper in my pocket. Dear Mother, I am the fairy princess you saw at the ball.

Mother. You, my dear! and I did not know you!

Herald. Now, lady, please come with me to the Prince's palace. You shall be a princess.

Cinderella. Good-by, dear sisters! Good-by, dear mother! I am going to the Prince's palace.

THE PIED PIPER

PERSONS IN THE PLAY—Mayor, First Councilman, Second Councilman, Third Councilman, Ten Citizens, Piper

Scene I.—*The Mayor's Office*

Mayor and Councilmen, sitting around a table.—Citizens come in.

First Citizen. Our Mayor is a noddy!

Second Citizen. Look at our corporation sitting in the gowns we pay for, and doing nothing!

Third Citizen. See here, how the rats made a nest in my Sunday hat!

Fourth Citizen. When I was cooking dinner the bold rats licked the soup from my ladle!

Fifth Citizen. They are so bold they are always fighting with the dogs and cats!

Sixth Citizen. Yes, and they kill them, too!

Seventh Citizen. My baby cried in his sleep, and when I went to him there was a big rat in his cradle.

Eighth Citizen. What are you going to do about it, Mr. Mayor?

Ninth Citizen. You'd better wake up, sirs! Don't go to sleep over this!

Tenth Citizen. I tell you, you'll have to do something to save us from this army of rats!

First Councilman. What *can* we do?

Second Councilman. I'm sure we've tried everything, but every day the rats grow worse and worse.

Third Councilman. I'm sure it isn't very pleasant for us to have the city overrun with the creatures!

Mayor. I'd sell my ermine gown for a guilder! It is no easy thing to be mayor and I wish I was a plowboy in the country! Try to think of something to do.

First Councilman. It is easy to bid us rack our own brains!

Second Councilman. I'm sure my head aches trying to think.

Third Councilman. I've wondered and thought, till I've no thoughts left.

Mayor. Oh! if I only had a great big trap! Yes, a thousand big traps! Bless us, what noise is that? Is it a rat?—Come in!

[*Enter Piper.*]

First Councilman. Who is this who dares to come into the Mayor's office without an introduction?

Second Councilman. Hasn't he a funny coat?

Third Councilman. But what a pleasant face! He smiles all the time.

Mayor. He looks like the picture of my grandsire. What is your name, and your business, my man?

Pied Piper. Please your honors, my name is Pied Piper. My business is to play upon my pipe. I can charm with the magic of my notes all things to do my will. But I use my charm on creatures that do people harm, the toad, the mole, and the viper, and rats—rats!

Mayor. Rats! Well, then, you're the man we want. We'll pay you a thousand guilders if you'll free our town of rats.

Piper. A thousand guilders! Done! It's a bargain!

Scene II.—*Same as Scene I. The Mayor and Councilmen looking out of window*

Mayor. There he goes down the street.

First Councilman. What a strange looking pipe he plays!

Second Councilman. I believe it must be a magic one.

Third Councilman. Do you hear the music? What is that other noise?

Mayor. Look, look at the rats! Did you ever see such a sight!

First Councilman. The streets are crowded with them! Big and little, brown, black, and gray, they are tumbling over each other in their hurry!

Second Councilman. Sir! he is going toward the bridge.

Third Councilman. They must think he is playing a tune of apples and cheese!

Mayor. There they are at the river. They are plunging in! they will be drowned!

First Councilman. Good for the piper!

Mayor. Ring the bells for the people. Tell them to get long poles, poke out the nests and block up the holes!

Second Councilman. Here comes the Piper.

Third Councilman. That was well done, Mr. Piper.

Pied Piper. Yes, all the rats are drowned and now I've come for my pay.

Mayor. Pay! why what have you done? Just played a tune on your pipe. You must be joking.

Piper. You promised—

First Councilman. You impudent fellow! You certainly don't think a tune on your pipe is worth one thousand guilders? There is no work in that.

Second Councilman. The rats are dead and can't come to life again, I think!

Mayor. My friend, we are much obliged, of course. We are much obliged and will gladly give you fifty guilders. You know your time is not worth more.

Piper. No trifling, pray. I'll have what you promised, or you may find that I'll play a tune you do not like!

Mayor. What! do you threaten us, fellow? Do what you please. Do you think we care? Play on your old pipe whatever tune you wish.

Piper. Listen, then, and look from your window when I play again in the street below.

[Goes out.]

Mayor. What does the lazy fellow mean by his threats?

First Councilman. Hear his wonderful music! Listen.

Second Councilman. Oh! what is he doing! See the children!

Third Councilman. They are following him. There is my son. Where are you going, my boy? Come back!

Mayor. Let me see! O woe! there are my own three lovely children. Run, some one, and stop them!

Third Councilman. I'll go; I'll go.

[*Runs out.*]

Mayor. It is useless. Every child in our city is following the magic sound.

Second Councilman. The music seems to say: "Come, children, to the wonderful land of play. There flowers and fruits will welcome you. The birds and beasts will play with you, and you will never be sad or sorry in the wonderful land of play." No wonder the children follow the Piper.

Third Councilman (*enters*). The children and the Piper have all disappeared! A mountain opened and let them in!

First Councilman. The children, the blessed children, have gone! What shall we do without the children?

Mayor. Oh, wicked man that I am! Why did I break my promise? Why did I not give him the thousand guilders?

Second Councilman. Yes, we are all wicked men, and we are punished for not keeping our word.

Mayor. Let us write this sad story on a column so that all may read; and let us paint the picture of the Piper with our little ones following him, on a church window, so that all men may know how our children have been stolen away.

First Councilman. And may this sad story teach us all to keep our word with every one.

MOTHER GOOSE'S PARTY

PERSONS IN THE PLAY—Mother Goose, Jack Goose, Mother Hubbard, Dog, A-Dillar-a-Dollar, Mary (and Her Lamb), Old Mrs. Shoeman, Her Sons (Tommy Tucker, Jacky Horner), Miss Muffet, Boy Blue, Bo-Peep, Nancy Etticoat, Little Boy Who Lives in the Lane, Old King Cole, Man in the Moon, Tom the Piper's Son, Mistress Mary

Scene I.—*Home of Mother Goose*

Mother Goose. I really think I must give a party. All my friends have been so good to me and I have been entertained in so many homes! Wherever I go I am sure to see one of my Mother Goose books, and the children all seem to love it so much. Let me see! whom shall I invite? I think I'll ask Old Mother Hubbard to take tea with me and we'll talk about the party together. Jack, Jack!

Jack (enters). Yes, mother dear, what is it?

Mother Goose. Jack Goose, I wish you to run over to Mother Hubbard's house and ask her to take tea with me this afternoon. Now be nimble, Jack,—be quick!

Jack. Yes, mother dear. See me jump over the candlestick! Isn't that fine jumping?

Mother Goose. Very fine indeed, Jack. Now do your errand, and hurry home.

Jack. Yes, mother, I will. Good-by.

Mother Goose. Good-by.

Scene II.—*House of Mother Hubbard*

Jack (knocking). I wonder if Old Mother Hubbard is at home. Hark! I hear her dog barking. Yes, and I hear her step. Here she is!

Mother Hubbard (opening the door). Who is this knocking so loud? Oh, it's you, little nimble Jack! Will you come in?

Jack. No, thank you, Mrs. Hubbard. My mother wishes you to come over to our house for tea this afternoon. Will you come?

Mother Hubbard. Yes, thank you, Jack, I will. Tell your mother that I'm just going to market to buy my poor doggie a bone.

Jack. O Mother Hubbard! *please* let me play with your dog. He's such a dear old doggie! Do you remember how he danced a jig the other day?

Mother Hubbard. Yes, Jack, I do; and I think you danced with him. You are both nimble young things and both like to dance. Well, good-by, now. Have a good time together and I'll bring you something little boys like.

Jack. Thank you! Good-by, good-by! Now, doggie, let's dance.

> Old Mother Hubbard, she went to the cupboard,
>   To get the poor doggie a bone;
> But when she got there, the cupboard was bare,
>   And so the poor doggie had none.

Dog (sadly). Bow-wow, bow-wow, bow-wow!

Jack. Oh! you don't like that song! Never mind, old fellow! Mother Hubbard has gone to the butcher's and she'll get you a bone, I'm sure. Wait till she comes back.

Dog (gayly). Bow-wow, bow-wow, bow-wow!

Jack. I thought you would like that. Here she comes now. We've had a lovely dance, Mother Hubbard, and now I must hurry home.

Mother Hubbard. Thank you for staying and taking good care of my dog. Here are some fresh Banbury buns for you.

Jack. Oh, thank you, Mother Hubbard. I'm very fond of Banbury buns. Good-by!

Mother Hubbard. Good-by, Jack. Tell your mother I'll be over soon.

Jack. Bring your dog with you, and we'll have another dance. Good-by.

Dog. Bow-wow! bow-wow! bow-wow!

Scene III.—*Mother Goose and Mother Hubbard at the Tea Table*

Mother Goose. I am pleased to see you, Mother Hubbard. I hear that your cupboard is no longer bare and empty, and I am very glad you are able to give your poor dog all the bones a good dog should have. Now for our tea. Shall I put two or three lumps in your cup?

Mother Hubbard. Three, please. I like my tea very sweet. And now tell me, Mother Goose, what is the reason you sent for me to-day?

Mother Goose. Well, I am going to give a party and I wish to ask your advice.

Mother Hubbard. Indeed! Whom do you think of inviting?

Mother Goose. First, the dear Old Woman who lives in the shoe—

Mother Hubbard. What! and all her children?

Mother Goose. No, only the two eldest. You know the party is for my son Jack, too, and we must have the young people as well as their parents. Old King Cole will come and bring his fiddlers three to play for the young folks who dance.

Mother Hubbard. I hope you won't invite Tom the Piper's Son, or My Son John as his mother calls him,—or Humpty-Dumpty. They are not good boys for your son Jack to play with!

Mother Goose. I suppose not; but I like them all, and I dislike to leave out anyone. I don't wish to hurt their feelings.

Mother Hubbard. There are little Bo-Peep and Boy Blue, who are good children, although rather silly; and there are little Miss Muffet and Nancy Etticoat, both very pretty little girls; and there are Jacky Horner and Tommy Tucker and the Man-in-the-Moon and Taffey and Daffey-Down-Dilly and—

Mother Goose. I'll have to give a garden party if I invite all those! I can't leave any out, and I think I'll have the party out-of-doors.

Mother Hubbard. That will be fine! I only hope it will be a pleasant day. When will you give it?

Mother Goose. Two weeks from to-day, the first of May.

Mother Hubbard. That's May Day and a very good day for a party out-of-doors. Well I must go home now. Good-by! If I can help you, please call upon me.

Mother Goose. Thank you, Mother Hubbard! Good-by, and thank you again for coming over.

SCENE IV.—*At the Party*

Mother Hubbard. What a lovely day you have for your party, Mother Goose! The sun shines so bright and warm, and the flowers are lovely. Is there anything I can do?

Mother Goose. No, thank you. I'm glad you came early. Have you seen the tables?

Mother Hubbard. They are lovely! Where did you get such pretty flowers?

Mother Goose. From Mistress Mary, quite contrary. You know she has a garden

With cockle shells, and silver bells,
And pretty maids all in a row.

Mother Hubbard. I see some one coming.

Mother Goose. Why, how do you do, A-Dillar-a-Dollar! Are you always in such good time?

A-Dillar-a-Dollar. I'm afraid not, Mrs. Goose. They call me

A ten o'clock scholar,
Why did you come so soon?
You used to come at ten o'clock,
And now you come at noon!

Mother Goose. And here comes Mary with her little lamb. Do you like the lamb better than a Teddy Bear, Mary?

Mary. Yes, indeed, I do. Because the lamb loves me, you know.

It followed me to school one day,
    Which was against the rule;
It made the children laugh and play,
    To see the lamb at school.

Mother Goose. Here comes the Old Woman who lives in a shoe, and her two oldest boys. Dear Mrs. Shoe-woman, I am very glad to see you! How did you leave all of your children?

Mrs. Shoe-woman. Oh, dear, Mother Goose! I have so many children I don't know what to do: when they are naughty I give them some broth without any bread, and whip them all soundly and put them to bed.

Mother Goose. Here are all the children coming to the party! Come, children, let us have a dance. All stand around the Maypole as I call your names:

Little Miss Muffet and Boy Blue;

Little Bo-Peep and Jacky Horner;

Nancy Etticoat and Jack-be-nimble;

Mary and the little Boy who lives in the Lane.

All take ribbons and stand around the Maypole. Are you all ready?

Children. Yes, Mother Goose, we are all ready when the music begins.

Mother Goose. Old King Cole, will you have your three fiddlers play for the dance?

King Cole. With pleasure, dear Mother Goose—and I'll sing:

Hey diddle, diddle! the cat and the fiddle;
    The cow jumped over the moon;
The little dog laughed to see such craft,
    And the dish ran away with the spoon.

Children (*sing*).

Old King Cole was a merry old soul;
    And a merry old soul was he;
He called for his pipe and he called for his bowl,
    And he called for his fiddlers three.

Mother Goose's Party

Mother Goose. These are very good songs, but they will not do for a Maypole dance. Here, Little Tommy Tucker, sing for your supper.

Tommy Tucker. All right, Mother Goose.

Handy Spandy, Jack-a-dandy,
    Loved plum cake and sugar candy;
He bought some at a grocer's shop,
    And out he came, hop, hop, hop.

Children.

Little Tommy Tucker, sings for his supper;
What shall he eat? White bread and butter;
How shall he eat it without any knife?
How shall he marry without any wife?

[*Dance about the Maypole.*]

Mother Goose. Why, who can that man be? He is tumbling down in a very queer way! Who are you?

Man.

I'm the Man in the Moon,
Come down too soon
To ask the way to Norwich.
I went by the south,
And burnt my mouth,
Eating cold pease-porridge.

Are Jack and Jill here?

Jack. Here I am, Mr. Moon-Man.

Jill. Oh, dear Mr. Moon-Man, where is your dog and your bundle of sticks?

Jack. Tell us what the children play in your country, the Moon!

Children. Please do, Mr. Moon-Man!

Moon-Man. Well, children, I can tell you how they learn to count. They all say—

One, two; buckle my shoe;
Three, four; shut the door;
Five, six; pick up sticks;

and then they all pick up sticks and put them on the fire.

Tom. I don't think that is much fun!

Children. Of course you don't. You don't like sticks.

Tom, Tom, the Piper's Son,
Stole a pig and away he run!
The pig was eat,
And Tom was beat,
And Tom ran roaring down the street!

Mistress Mary. Now, children, let us sit in a circle and play games and sing songs. Little Bo-Peep, you may sing your little song first.

Little Bo-Peep.

> Little Bo-Peep, she lost her sheep,
>   And doesn't know where to find them;

Children.

> Leave them alone and they will come home
>   Bringing their tails behind them.

Mistress Mary. Now Jack and Jill—

Jack and Jill. Shall we go up the hill to get a pail of water?

Children.

> Jack and Jill went up the hill
>   To get a pail of water.
> Jack fell down and broke his crown,
>   And Jill came tumbling after.

Boys.

> Up Jack got and home did trot
>   As fast as he could caper;
> He went to bed to mend his head,
>   With vinegar and brown paper.

Girls.

> Jill came in and she did grin,
>   To see his paper plaster;
> Her mother, vexed, did spank her next
>   For laughing at Jack's disaster.

Mistress Mary. Now, I'll sing a song and then help Mother Goose with the supper. [*Sings.*]

> Sing a song a sixpence,
>   Pocket full of rye;
> Four-and-twenty blackbirds
>   Baked in a pie.
> When the pie was opened
>   The birds began to sing,
> Wasn't that a dainty dish
>   To set before the king?

Mother Goose. Now I must have some children to help me.

Jack Goose. I'll take the bean porridge hot and bean porridge cold, mother, and Tommy Tucker can go with me and pass the white bread and butter.

Mother Goose. That's my good Jack. Now Tom the Piper's Son may take the roast pig and Mary may pass the Banbury cross buns.

Miss Muffet. Dear Mother Goose, may I pass the curds and whey?

Mother Goose. Yes, my dear child, but be careful not to spill any. Then for the last course Jack Horner will pass the Christmas pie and give every child a big fat plum.

Children (sing).

> Little Jacky Horner
> Sitting in a corner
> Eating a Christmas pie
> He put in his thumb
> And pulled out a plum
> And said—What a great boy am I?

Old King Cole. Mother Goose, you have given us a beautiful party and we have had a lovely time. We hope you will live to give many more to your friends and the children.

Children. Yes, Mother Goose, your party was just lovely!

Mother Goose. Thank you, dear children.

King Cole. Now, little folks, let us sing a good-by song to Mother Goose.

The girls (bowing to King Cole).

> The king was in the counting room,
> Counting out his money.

The boys (bowing to Mother Goose).

> The queen was in the parlor,
> Eating bread and honey.

All.

> The maid was in the garden

(To Mistress Mary)

> Hanging out the clothes,
> Along came a blackbird
> And nipped off her nose!

Mother Goose. And that story means that night is coming and putting the day to sleep.

King Cole. So it does, and you see the sun is fast going down behind the western hills. Say good-by, children, for it is time to go home.

Children. Good night, Mother Goose.

Mother Goose. Good night, dear children, and don't forget your old Mother Goose.

Children. Forget dear Mother Goose? Never! Good-by, good-by!

Mother Goose. Good-by.

LITTLE TWO-EYES

PERSONS IN THE PLAY—Mother, Little One-Eye, Little Two-Eyes, Little Three-Eyes, Little Old Woman, Tree, Prince, Goat

Scene I.—*Dining Room at Little Two-Eyes' Home*

Mother. Come to dinner, little One-Eye and little Three-Eyes. Here is some good soup and white bread for you. Little Two-Eyes, you can have what your sisters do not want.

Little Three-Eyes. Here's a crust for you. That is enough for a girl with only two eyes.

Little One-Eye. What a shame to have a sister with two eyes! You look just like other people! Little Three-Eyes and I are very different.

Little Three-Eyes. Here little Two-Eyes, take this bowl. I don't want any more and you can have what is left.

Mother. Now, children, run away and play. Little Two-Eyes, take the goat and go out to the hillside. You must stay till it begins to get dark, and then you may come home. You must work, because you have two eyes like other people, but my little One-Eye and Three-Eyes may stay at home and play.

Scene II.—*On the Hillside*

Little Two-Eyes. Come, little goat, here is some green grass for you to eat. I wish that my sisters loved me and that my mother was not ashamed of me. Oh, why do I have two eyes just like all other people? I am so hungry, Oh, dear! Oh, dear! (*Cries.*)

Wood Fairy. My child, why do you cry?

Little Two-Eyes. Because I have only two eyes, and my mother and my sisters treat me badly. I don't have enough to eat and I am so hungry. My dress is old, and my sisters have nice dresses and pretty ribbons. But who are you?

Wood Fairy. I am the little Old Woman who lives on this hill. I have come to help you. Listen, little Two-Eyes! You need never be hungry again. Say to your little goat:

44

Little goat, bleat!
Little table, rise!

Then a table will rise before you with all the food you can eat. When you have finished eating, you must say:

Little goat, bleat!
Little table, away!

and it will disappear before your eyes. Good-by, dear little Two-Eyes. I must go now, but remember what I have told you.

Little Two-Eyes. Why, where has that queer looking little woman gone? I am so hungry I'll try now if what she said can be true.

Little goat, bleat!
Little table, rise!

Goat. Bla-a! Bla-a! Bla-a!

Little Two-Eyes. Oh, look, little goat! what a pretty table! and how good the food looks. Now we shall have all we want to eat. Here is something for you, and here are oranges and meat and pudding for me! Dear little woman! How can I thank her? Now I can eat no more.

Little goat, bleat!
Little table, away!

Goat. Bla-a! Bla-a! Bla-a!

Little Two-Eyes. There, it is gone. Aren't we happy, little goat? But see, it is time to go home. Come, little goat.

Scene III.—*At Home*

Mother. Here, little Two-Eyes, here are the crusts your sisters saved for you.

Two-Eyes. Thank you, mother, but I don't care for any crusts. I'm not hungry.

Mother. Not care for them? You are not hungry? You have always eaten them before now and asked for more! You didn't eat any supper last night, either. What does this mean? What did you have to eat to-day?

Two-Eyes. I cannot tell you, mother.

Mother. You cannot? Then, little One-Eye, you shall go to the hillside with little Two-Eyes and find out why she is no longer hungry.

Little One-Eye. I don't want to go! The walk is too long, and I shall get tired!

Mother. Just this once, my dear! You will not have to go again. But we must learn the secret.

Little Two-Eyes. Come, sister. Come, little goat.

Scene IV.—*The Hillside*

Little Two-Eyes. Now we are almost there. Are you tired, little One-Eye?

Little One-Eye. Oh! I am so tired, and my feet hurt so I can hardly walk.

Little Two-Eyes. I have to walk this far every day.

Little One-Eye. Yes, but you have two eyes like other people and you must expect to work. I cannot go any farther. I'll lie down here and rest.

Little Two-Eyes. I'll sing you a pretty song:

> Are you awake, little One-Eye?
> Are you asleep, little One-Eye?

Yes, you are asleep, little One-Eye, and now I can have my dinner.

> Little goat, bleat!
> Little table, rise!

Goat. Bla-a! Bla-a! Bla-a!

Little Two-Eyes. Here is the little table again! Oh, how thankful I am for the good food. Dear little old woman, you are very good to send me such nice things to eat. Here is some for you, little goat. Now I have had enough.

> Little goat, bleat!
> Little table, away!

There, it is gone. Little One-Eye, wake up! It is time to go home.

Little One-Eye. Did I go to sleep?

Little Two-Eyes. Indeed, you did, and now we must hurry home. Come, little goat!

Scene V.—*At Home*

Mother. Well, little One-Eye, tell us what you have seen. Why doesn't little Two-Eyes eat the food we have for her?

Little One-Eye. I don't know, mother. The way was so long and I was so tired; I fell asleep; and when I woke up it was time to come home.

Mother. It was a hard walk for you, my dear; but we must find out who is giving little Two-Eyes something to eat. To-morrow you must go, little Three-Eyes.

Little Three-Eyes. I'll find out, mother. If anyone dares to give food to little Two-Eyes, I'll tell you all about it.

Mother. Yes, my dear, I know you won't go to sleep. I can trust you to find out everything.

SCENE VI.—*On the Hillside*

Little Two-Eyes. Come, sister, we must go on, for it is a long way to the top of the hill.

Little Three-Eyes. I'm not going any farther, I'm too tired! I'll rest a little here.

Little Two-Eyes. All right, little Three-Eyes. I'll sing you a song.

> Are you awake, little Three-Eyes?
> Are you asleep, little Two-Eyes?

Yes, you are asleep, and now I'll have my dinner.

> Little goat, bleat!
> Little table, rise!

Goat. Bla-a! Bla-a! Bla-a!

Little Two-Eyes. Here is our dinner again, little goat. See this fresh lettuce and cabbage and good bread and butter. Here is some honey, too, and cake. Isn't this a good dinner?

> Little goat, bleat!
> Little table, away!

Goat. Bla-a, bla-a, bla-a!

Little Two-Eyes. Now it is gone. Three-Eyes, wake up! It is time home.

Little Three-Eyes. How long I have slept! What will my mother say? But I think I have a surprise for you, little Two-Eyes!

SCENE VII.—*At Home*

Mother. Well, little Three-Eyes, did you go to sleep, too?

Little Three-Eyes.—Yes, mother, but only with two eyes. Little Two-Eyes sang to me,

"Are you awake, little Three-Eyes?
Are you asleep, little Two-Eyes?"

and so two of my eyes went to sleep, but one stayed awake and watched.

Mother. What did you see? Tell me quickly, dear little Three-Eyes.

Little Three-Eyes. First she said,

"Little goat, bleat!
Little table, rise!"

and the goat said, "Bla-a, bla-a, bla-a!" Then a table came up out of the ground. Oh! it was such a pretty little table with a white cloth over it and all kinds of good things on it. No wonder little Two-Eyes doesn't eat any of our common food. It isn't good enough for her! She has food fit for a queen,— nuts and cake, and candy, too!

Mother. So that is why little Two-Eyes doesn't eat the crusts we save for her! Well, I'll see if she is going to have better food, than we have. Bring me the long sharp knife.

[*Goes out and soon returns.*]

There, now the goat is dead. Little Two-Eyes, perhaps you'll eat the food we give you now!

Little Two-Eyes. Oh, my poor little goat! What shall I do without it!

Mother. Go to bed, and to-morrow morning you shall go to the hillside alone. And you must stay there all day, too.

SCENE VIII.—*On the Hillside*

Little Two-Eyes. Oh, dear! Oh, dear! my poor goat is dead! Now I shall be hungry and lonely too! Where shall I go, and what can I do?

Little Wood Fairy. Little Two-Eyes, why are you weeping?

Little Two-Eyes. Because my mother has killed my poor goat, and she has sent me here to stay all alone, and I am so hungry and thirsty again.

Little Wood Fairy. Little Two-Eyes, let me tell you what to do. Ask your sisters to give you the heart of your goat. Bury it in the ground before the house door. Watch, and to-morrow a wonderful tree will come up out of the ground.

Little Two-Eyes. Thank you, dear little woman! I'll go home and do as you have told me.

SCENE IX.—*At Home*

Little Two-Eyes. Little One-Eye and little Three-Eyes, please let me have the heart of my goat!

One-Eye. Certainly, if that is all you want.

Three-Eyes. Here it is, but I don't see what you want it for!

Little Two-Eyes (*goes to door*). Now I'll plant it as the little woman told me. I wonder what kind of a tree will appear to-morrow? Poor little goat, I'm so sorry you have gone! Now I must go into the house and try to sleep.

SCENE X.—*In the Garden*

Little One-Eye. Mamma, mamma, look here! Come quickly! Isn't this a wonderful tree!

Mother. Why, how strange! This tree was not here yesterday. I wonder how it came! I never saw such a beautiful tree before!

Little One-Eye. Do you see the golden apples on it? O mamma! may we have some? Please, mother!

Mother. Yes, dear little One-Eye. You are the oldest, climb up into the tree and pick some golden apples for us.

One-Eye. That will be fun. Here I go!

Mother. Why don't you get the apples, little One-Eye?

Little One-Eye. They all get away from me. When I try to pick one it springs back!

Mother. Come down, little One-Eye. Now little Three-Eyes, you can see better with your three eyes, than your sister with her one eye. You may climb up and get some apples for us.

Little Three-Eyes. I'll pick a lot of them and throw them down for you to catch. Why, how funny they act! I almost get one and it always springs away!

Mother. Come down and let me try. I never heard of fruit that would not be picked. Now children, I'll get some of the lovely apples for you. There! Why, what is the matter? I can't reach a single apple.

Little Two-Eyes. Let me try; perhaps I can pick some.

Mother. You, with your two eyes! How can you expect to get them if we can't?

Little Two-Eyes. Please let me try, mother.

Mother. Well, I suppose you can try, but I know you can't get them.

Two-Eyes. Here they are. Catch them, mother; catch them, little One-Eye! Oh, mother! I see a young man on horseback coming along the road. He looks like a prince.

Mother. Hurry down, little Two-Eyes! He must not see you,—a girl with two eyes! I'm ashamed of you. Hide under this barrel!

[*The prince rides up.*]

Prince. Good morning, ladies, what a lovely tree you have here! She who gives me a branch shall have whatever she wishes.

Little One-Eye. The tree is ours, Great Prince; but when we try to get its fruit, it slips away from us.

Prince. It is strange, if the tree belongs to you, that you cannot get the fruit! But where do these apples come from?

Little Three-Eyes. We have another sister, but she has only two eyes and we are ashamed of her; so we hid her under this barrel, and she has rolled the apples out to you.

Prince. Little Two-Eyes, come out. Can you get me a branch from this wonderful tree?

Little Two-Eyes. Yes, Prince; here is a branch with many golden apples on it.

Prince. And what is your wish, little Two-Eyes?

Little Two-Eyes. O Prince! My mother and my sisters are ashamed of me and do not treat me well. They do not give me enough to eat and they do not like to have me near them. Please take me away where I can be happy and free!

Prince. Come with me, little Two-Eyes; you shall go to my father's palace and be a little princess. There you will be happy and free and never be hungry or lonely again.

THE DAYS OF THE WEEK

THE WEEK—Monday, Tuesday, Wednesday, Thursday, Friday, Saturday, Sunday

Monday. Well, I am glad to be here at last. Certainly my work is very important. As the first working day of the week, I begin all business; and I have always heard that if a thing is well begun, it is half done. People call me Moon-day—isn't that a pretty name, the day of the moon? How beautiful the moon is, riding in her silver chariot across the dark blue sky! I am proud of my name. The moon is constantly changing and I like change. I like brightness and cleanliness too, and good housewives wash their clothes on Monday. How white and clean they look hanging on the line! The sun and wind play hide and seek and help to cleanse the clothes. School begins on Monday and the little children run and laugh on their way to school. Every one seems happy that another week has begun.

Tuesday. I am named for Tui, the god of war. In the countries of the north I am greatly honored by all the people. Soldiers when going to war call on Tui for help, and they like to begin a battle on Tuesday. Monday likes to begin work, but I like to make some progress. The children always know their lessons better on Tuesday, and are happier than on Monday. The white clothes are sprinkled and rolled, and now the maids iron the pretty baby dresses and the house linen. They sing and laugh over their work. The world is all running smoothly on Tuesday, and I think I like my work the best.

Wednesday. I should be the best of days, for I am named for Woden, or Odin, the king of the gods. The hardest work of the week is finished when I come, and there is time for a rest. Perhaps mother will bake a special cake for dinner. To-day the children take their music lessons, and the boys go for a lesson in swimming or gymnastic exercise. This is the day young people choose for their wedding day, and you don't know how glad I am to be a part of their happiness. I believe I have more sunshine than the other days, for Woden likes to have clear skies and health-giving breezes. I would not change with any of my sister days.

Thursday. I bring the thunder and the lightning, and I cleave the dark clouds with my rapid flashes. I glory in a storm, for Thor, the god of thunder, has chosen me for his day, and I bear his name. A life of ease and quiet has no charms for me. I like the din and crash of war, the noise and hurry of business. The fury of the heavens, the crash of falling trees, the roaring of waters,—what can give greater pleasure? Business thrives on Thursday. Men rush to and fro, buying and selling, building great houses, digging in the mines, and sailing the seas. Life and action are my delight. Hurrah for Thor's day!

Friday. After the bustle and work of the week I come to clean and settle all disturbances. Now dirt and dust must disappear under the broom and brush.

How the windows shine and how spotless is the hearth! Children rake up the leaves and burn them; all rubbish must be cleared away. Order and neatness I love; and so does Freya, for whom I am named. She is the goddess of beauty, and there is no beauty where neatness and order are absent. Some say that I am an unlucky day, but that is a mistake. See what wonderful things have happened on my day, what great men have been born on Friday! I am the last school day of the week, and to-day the children may forget lessons and play outdoors a little longer. To-day the family gather for a story at the twilight hour, and all is rest and happiness.

Saturday. I am the jolly day of the week. "School is out!" the children cry, and all day long they sing and call to each other in their games. To-day I smell the cakes and pies cooking in the range, for Saturday is baking day. How the little children love to watch mother stirring the cake and frosting, and how they beg to clean the sweet stuff out of the bowl. Father comes home earlier to-day, and all go for a walk in the woods or park. All men need a holiday, for "all work and no play makes Jack a dull boy." The boys play ball and run and shout in their joy. The girls have little parties, and cook gives them some fresh cakes. I am named for Saetere, god of the harvest, and he is always merry. So I wish all people to be happy on Saturday, the play day of the week.

Sunday. You have all spoken well, my sisters, and each one has some claim to be the best day of the week. How fine it is that every day holds some special joy in work or play! But you all know the highest joy is mine. I am named for the golden sun that gives light to the world. On Sunday men think of the inner light that makes them love the good and the true and persuades them to do right. To-day the family is united, and in the morning with fresh garments and happy faces they seek the knowledge of a higher life. Around the dinner table they talk happily together of their work and play, and they plan how they may do better work during the next week. Love and peace are in all hearts. A desire to help the weak and poor and sad is in every soul. I am happy and blest to be Sunday.

HÄNSEL AND GRETEL

PERSONS IN THE PLAY—Hänsel, Gretel, Mother, Father, The Gingerbread Witch, Sandman, Children

Scene I.—*In the Cottage*

Hänsel. I wish mother would come home! I'm cold and hungry. I'm tired of bread. I want some milk and sugar.

Gretel. Hush, Hänsel; don't be cross!

Hänsel. If we only had something good to eat: eggs, and butter and meat. Oh, dear!

Gretel. Dear Hänsel, if you will stop crying, I'll tell you a secret.

Hänsel. Oh, what is it? Something nice?

Gretel. Yes, indeed. Look in this jug! It is full of milk. Mother will make us a pudding for supper.

Hänsel. Goody, goody! How thick the cream is! Let me taste it.

Gretel. Aren't you ashamed, you naughty boy! Take your finger out of the cream. We must go back to work. When mother comes she will be cross if you have not finished the broom.

Hänsel. I'll not work any more. I want to dance.

Gretel. So do I. I like to dance better than to work. Come, let us dance and sing.

> Brother, come and dance with me,
> Both my hands I offer thee;
> > Right foot first,
> > Left foot then,
> Round about and back again.

Hänsel. I can't dance. Show me what I ought to do.

Gretel. Look at me. Do this.

> With your foot you tap, tap, tap!
> With your hands you clap, clap, clap!
> > Right foot first,
> > Left foot then,

Round about and back again.

Hänsel (*dancing*).

With your hands you clap, clap, clap!
With your foot you tap, tap, tap!
Right foot first,
Left foot then,
Round about and back again.

Gretel. That is fine, brotherkin! Soon you will dance as well as I. Come, try again.

With your head you nick, nick, nick!
With your fingers click, click, click!
Right foot first,
Left foot then,
Round about and back again.

Hänsel.

O Gretel dear, O sister dear,
Come dance and sing with me.

Gretel.

O Hänsel dear, O brother dear,
Come dance and sing with me.
Tra, la, la, tra, la, la,
La, la, la, la, tra, la, la.

[*Knocks down the milk.*]

Mother (*enters*). What is all this noise?

Gretel. 'Twas Hänsel. He wanted—

Hänsel. 'Twas Gretel. She said I—

Mother. Hush, you noisy children! What work have you done? Gretel, your stocking is not done yet; and where are your brooms, you lazy Hans? You have knocked over the milk too! What shall we have for supper? Lazy folks can't stay in my house. Take the basket and go to the woods for strawberries. And don't dare to come back without them! Off with you! and be quick too!

[*The children go out. Mother sits weeping.*]

Oh! I am so tired and hungry. Nothing in the house to eat. What shall I do for the poor hungry children—Oh, dear, what can I do!

[*Goes to sleep, crying.*]

Father (*enters, singing*).

Hillo, hilloo, hillo, hilloo,
Little mother, where are you?

Mother (*looking up*). Who is singing and making so much noise?

Father. I called you, for I am hungry and want my supper.

Mother. Your supper! with nothing in the house to eat and nothing to drink.

Father. Let us see. Open your eyes and look in my basket. Cheer up, mother!

Mother. What do I see? Ham and butter and flour and sausage! Where did you get all these good things, father?

Father. Hurrah, won't we have a merry time, won't we have a happy time? I sold so many brooms at the fair that I could buy you all these good things and some tea besides.

Mother. Tea! how good it smells and how glad I am! Now I will cook the supper.

Father. But where are the children? Hänsel! Gretel! Where are they?

Mother. Oh, the bad children! They did no work and they were singing and dancing and spilled the milk, so I sent them to the woods to pick some strawberries for supper.

Father. Laughing and dancing! Why should you be angry? Where have they gone?

Mother. To the mountain.

Father. To the mountain! the home of the witch!

Mother. What do you mean? The witch?

Father. Yes, the old witch of the mountain turns all children to gingerbread and then she eats them.

Mother. Eats them! Oh, my children, my pretty little children! Come, we must find them! Hänsel, Gretel, where are you?

[*Runs out.*]

Father. I will go with you, mother. Don't cry! we will surely find them.

[*Goes out.*]

SCENE II.—*In the Forest*

HÄNSEL, GRETEL

Gretel. See, my wreath is nearly done.

Hänsel. And the basket is filled with strawberries. Won't mother be pleased? We will have them for supper.

Gretel. Let me put the wreath on you!

Hänsel. No, no! boys don't wear wreaths. Put it on your own head. You shall be queen of the woods.

Gretel. Then I must have a nosegay, too.

Hänsel. Now you have a scepter and a crown. You shall have some strawberries, too. Don't they taste good?

Gretel. Let me feed you.

Hänsel. And I'll feed you. Don't be greedy!

Gretel. Oh, Hänsel, the berries are all gone. What naughty children we are! We must pick some more now for mother.

Hänsel. I don't care, I was so hungry. But it is too late to pick strawberries now. Let us go home.

Gretel. Let us hurry; it is dark and I'm afraid.

Hänsel. Pooh, *I'm* not afraid. But I can't see the way. Gretel, we're lost!

Gretel. What was that?

Hänsel. What?

Gretel. That shining there in the dark!

Hänsel. Pshaw, don't be afraid! That is a birch tree in its silver dress.

Gretel. There, see! a lantern is coming this way.

Hänsel. That is a will-of-the-wisp with its little candle.

Gretel. I'm frightened, I'm frightened! I wish I were home!

Hänsel. Gretelkin, stick close to me! I'll take care of you.

Gretel. See! what is that little man in gray?

Hänsel. I see him, too. I wonder who he is!

Sandman (comes).

> With my little bag of sand
> By every child's bedside I stand.
> Then little tired eyelids close,
> And little limbs have sweet repose.
> Then from the starry sphere above
> The angels come with peace and love.
> Then slumber, children, slumber,
> For happy dreams are sent you
> Through the hours you sleep.
>
> [*Goes away.*]

Hänsel. I'm sleepy. Let us go to sleep.

Gretel. Let us say our prayers first.

Both.

> When at night I go to sleep
> Fourteen angels watch do keep:
> Two my head are guarding,
> Two my feet are guiding,
> Two are on my right hand,
> Two are on my left hand,
> Two who warmly cover,
> Two who o'er me hover,
> Two to whom 'tis given
> To guide my steps to Heaven.

Gretel. Good night, dear brother.

Hänsel. Good night, dear sister. Don't be afraid. I'll take care of you.

[*They sleep.*]

SCENE III.—*In the Wood—Morning*

Hänsel. Wake up, dear little sister! The birds are singing and it is time to get up!

Gretel. I'm awake, dear brother. Come, let us hurry home.

Hänsel. Here is a path! Oh, Gretel, look at the pretty house!

Gretel. A cottage all made of chocolate creams!

Hänsel. The house seems to smile!

Gretel. It looks good enough to eat.

Hänsel. Let's nibble it!

[*A voice within the house.*]

Nibble, nibble, manikin!
Who's nibbling at my housekin?

Hänsel. Oh, did you hear?

Gretel. It's the wind!

Hänsel. Never mind, let us eat the cake. I'm hungry. Take a bite! Isn't it good?

Gretel. Yes, and look at the candy! What a funny fence this is! It looks like little boys and girls made of gingerbread with sugar trimmings. I wonder who lives in this house?

[*The Gingerbread Woman comes out of the house and speaks.*]

You've come to visit me, that is sweet,
You charming children, so good to eat!

Hänsel. Who are you, ugly one? Let me go!

Gretel. Take your arms away from me!

The Gingerbread Witch. Come into my house, little children! You may have sugarplums and peaches and cherries and candies and everything nice that little folks like!

Hänsel. No, I won't! I don't want to go into your house. I want to go home!

Gretel. I don't like you, Mrs. Gingerbread! You aren't nice like my mother. I want to go home to my own mother!

The Gingerbread Witch. Come, dear little Gretel. You must go in with me. We'll leave Hänsel in this little house outside. He must get fatter, so we will give him many good things to eat. Get in, Hänsel. I must lock you in!

Hänsel. What are you going to do with me?

The Gingerbread Witch. I'll fatten you up nicely and then you will see! Now I'll go inside for some sugarplums. You wait here, Gretel, until I come back. Hocus, pocus, malus locus! now you can't move!

[*Goes in.*]

Hänsel. Listen, Gretel! Watch the old witch and see everything she does to me. Hush, she's coming back!

The Gingerbread Witch. Now, Hans, eat this raisin. It will make you fat! Now,

Gretel, you have stood still long enough.

Hocus, pocus, elder bush!
Rigid body loosen, hush!

Then, Gretel, you must come with me, but Hans cannot move until he gets nice and fat like you. Run in, little daughter, and get some more nuts and raisins for him. I like plump little bodies like yours!

[Gretel goes in.]

Hänsel. Please let me out, Mrs. Gingerbread.

The Gingerbread Witch. When you are fatter. Now I must look to my fire. It is burning well, and the oven will soon be hot enough to bake my dinner. When I change my gingerbread I'll pop little Gretel in and shut the door.

[Gretel comes in very quietly and goes to Hans.]

Gretel.

Hocus, pocus, elder bush!
Rigid body loosen, hush!

The Gingerbread Witch. What are you saying?

Gretel. Oh, nothing,—only,—

The Gingerbread Witch. Only what?

Gretel. Only, much good may it do to Hans!

The Gingerbread Witch. Poor Hans is too thin, but I hope the raisins and nuts will be good for him. But, you, my plump little Gretel, are just fat enough— come, peep in the oven and see if the gingerbread is ready!

Hänsel (softly).

Sister dear, have a care;
She means to hurt you, so beware!

Gretel (shyly). I don't understand what I am to do!

The Gingerbread Witch. Do? Why, open the oven door!

Hänsel. Sister dear, now take care!

Gretel. I'm such a goose, I don't understand.

The Gingerbread Witch. Do as I say, it's only play! This is the way.

[Opens the door and looks in oven. Hans and Gretel run and push her in.]

Children sing. One little push, bang goes the door, clang! Now, let us be happy, dancing so merrily. Hurrah! Hurrah!

Hänsel. Why, see the children, Gretel. The fence is moving! The gingerbread children are *real* children, but their eyes are shut!

The Children. We are saved! We are saved!

Gretel. Who are you? Why do you keep your eyes shut? You're sleeping and yet you are talking!

The Children. O touch us, we pray, that we may awake!

Hänsel. The witch has changed them into gingerbread children. I know what to do. Let us say what the witch said to you, and what you said to me!

Hänsel and Gretel.

Hocus, pocus, elder bush!
Rigid body loosen, hush!

The Children. (Opening their eyes and running toward Hänsel and Gretel.) We thank you, we thank you both!

Gretel. Oh, I am so glad!

The Children. The spell is broken and we are free. The witch can do us no more harm. Come, let us shout for glee!

Hänsel.

Come, children all, and form a ring,
Join hands together, while we sing.

Gretel. Oh, Hänsel dear, I wish father and mother were here!

Hänsel. Look, Gretel! There they are!

[*Father and Mother enter.*]

Father. Why, mother, the children are here! Come, my dear Hänsel and Gretel! How glad I am we have found you safe and well!

Hänsel. Oh, father, we must tell you all about the Gingerbread Witch!

Mother. My dear children, were you frightened?

Gretel. Yes, mother, I was. But, mother, Hänsel comforted me, and we said our prayers and went to sleep.

Mother. The good angels watched over you and brought you back! Come, let us go to the village and take all these dear children to their mothers. Won't they be surprised and happy to see their dear children again?

Father. Come, children!

KING ALFRED

PERSONS IN THE PLAY—Queen Judith, Ethelbald, Ethelbert, Ethelred, Alfred, Peasants, King's Officers

Scene I.—*In the Castle*

Ethelbald. Tell us a story, lady mother.

Ethelbert. Yes, tell us a story.

Ethelred. I wish it would stop raining, so that we might take our hawks for a hunt!

Queen. I have something to show you, my princes. Is not this a beautiful book?

Alfred. How lovely the red velvet, and see, the clasp is of gold!

Ethelred. And there are jewels in the clasp!

Queen. It is well bound, as so precious a volume should be; but the binding is the least valuable part of the book. Shall we look within?

Ethelbald. Pray show us, lady mother!

Queen. Observe the forms of mighty warriors, fair ladies, and royal chiefs of the olden times in bright and glowing colors.

Ethelbert. How brave they look! Who are they? Tell us of them, dear mother.

Queen. These pictures are beautiful and appeal to the eye, but neither they nor the velvet and gold of the binding give the joy which is greatest.

Alfred. What do you mean, dear lady mother?

Queen. This is a book I greatly enjoy, for it is full of the tales of the mighty King Arthur and his Knights of the Round Table. You will like to hear me read these brave stories when you are tired with your day's work, or on rainy days when you can neither hunt nor ride. Then you know not how to amuse yourselves and time is heavy on your hands, since you can neither read nor play upon the musical instruments that give us so much pleasure.

Ethelred. The book is so lovely. Let me take it, lady mother!

Queen. I would that the children of my royal husband could read the book.

Ethelbald. Our father does not think much of books and music. He likes to hunt and fight, and so do I.

Ethelred. And I love to hunt, but I love to hear the stories of great kings and warriors, too.

Alfred. To which of us wilt thou give the book, lady mother?

Queen. I will bestow it on him who shall first learn how to read it.

Alfred. Will you really, dear mother?

Queen. Yes, upon the faith of a queen, I will. I will not give it to one who cannot read it. Books are meant for the learned and not for the ignorant. The sons of a king should cease to play with toys.

Alfred. May I take the book a little while?

Queen. Yes, you may take the precious volume, Alfred, for I know you will not injure it, and I hope you will soon learn how to make its wisdom your own.

Alfred. Thank you, lady mother. I shall study the book and learn to read, for I wish to know all about the brave knights of Arthur's court.

Scene II.—*Years later, when Alfred is King*

King Alfred, Oscar the Earl, Odulph, the Earl's Son

Alfred. All the others have gone back to their homes. In no other way can ye serve me. Wherefore do ye go about to weep and break my heart?

Oscar. We weep, royal Alfred, because thou hast forbidden us to share thy fortunes; as if we were the swarm of summer flies, who follow only while the sun shineth.

Alfred. My valiant Oscar, and you my faithful Odulph, listen to me. I do not despair. The time is not ripe now for further war. Our foes the Danes have conquered us for a time. I trust that the time will come when we shall drive them from our land. But we must do that which seems best for the present and seek to be more successful in the future. We must not sit down and weep; no, this rather shall you do. Go back to your own people and keep me in their memory. When the Dane rules most cruelly, then rise up and cry aloud in the ears of the people, "Alfred the king yet liveth!" Then gather the soldiers and I shall come to lead them to victory.

Oscar. Thou shalt be obeyed, my royal lord. I will return to my men and do as thou hast said. But let my son Odulph stay with thee, if only as thy servant.

Odulph. Well will I serve thee, my royal lord. It is not well for the king to fare alone.

Alfred. I am well content to serve myself, or even to be servant to others, until a happier time shall come. If Odulph desires to serve me, it shall be by bringing good tidings of your success with my people. When the time comes that we may again fight for our country, let him bring me the welcome message. Then we will free our country from the Danish yoke.

Oscar. Farewell, my royal master, since thou wilt have it so.

Odulph. And may the time soon come when I shall bring the message to thee!

Alfred. Farewell, my loyal friends. All will be well.

SCENE III.—*In the Peasant's Home*

KING ALFRED, PEASANT CUDRED, WIFE SWITHA

Alfred. Save you, good father! May a Saxon stranger, whom the Danish robbers have made homeless, share a lodging with thy master's cattle for the night?

Cudred. Wilt thou swear to me that thou art not a Dane in disguise?

Alfred. I say to thee, my friend, I am no Dane, but a true Saxon.

Cudred. Then thou shalt share the calf's crib to-night. Perchance thou art hungry, too?

Alfred. To say truth, father, I have not broken my fast to-day; neither have I had aught to drink save from these marshy streams. I shall be right thankful for some food, even a crust of coarsest rye bread.

Cudred. Rye bread, forsooth! Thou talkest of dainties indeed! Thou wilt get nothing better than flat oaten cakes here.

Alfred. I have always wished to taste an oaten cake.

Cudred. Follow me, then, and thou shalt have thy desire. Switha, Switha!

Switha. Well, I hear thee!

Cudred. Switha, I have brought thee home a guest who will be glad to partake of our supper.

Switha. A guest! And thinkest thou I've naught better to do than broil fish and bake cakes for all the vagabonds who roam the land?

Cudred. Patience, good Switha. I have not asked thee to cook for a vagabond. This is an honest Saxon whom it will be charity to feed and shelter for the night.

Switha. Let me hold the torch and see this Saxon guest. Thou lookest like a guest of fashion, sorry fellow!

Cudred. Cease thy scolding talk, woman! I see by this light that our guest hath not been used to beg for charity from such as thou. Why be so hard of heart and by thy rude taunts make bitter the food he must receive from our hands?

Switha. I have heard that charity begins at home, and I am sure we are poor enough.

Cudred. Not poor enough to refuse food to the hungry, such as it is. Here is fish, and here an oaten cake which you wish to taste.

Alfred. Thanks for your goodness, kind host. Indeed, I am hungry.

Switha. You eat like a hungry wolf.

Alfred. And now I am hungry no longer. I thank you both for a good supper, and I hope you will never be sorry you have given charity to a stranger. Now, Cudred, I shall be glad to sleep.

Cudred. This way, then, to the bed of straw. Now, tell me truly, art thou not some mighty earl in disguise?

Alfred. I am Alfred, thy king—I know from thy goodness to me when thou thoughtest me a beggar that thou art a good man, therefore I confide in thee. I know thou wilt not betray thy king.

Cudred. Not all the gold of Denmark should tempt me to commit so base a crime, but we must not let Switha know who thou art, my royal master.

Alfred. I shall be careful. Soon, I hope, my friends will bring me word that my army awaits me, when I shall again try to set my country free.

Scene IV.—*In the Peasant's Hut*

King Alfred, Switha

King Alfred. It rains so hard to-day that I cannot hunt, so will mend my bow and make some new arrows. May I sit by your fire, good dame Switha?

Switha. Yes, and as I have made a good batch of cakes you might watch them bake.

Alfred. Gladly will I watch them. Show me what I must do.

Switha. Turn them often before the fire, thus, so that they will not burn. Now I will go for more wood for the fire.

Alfred. How long, I wonder, must I remain in hiding. It is very hard to wait. If only I knew how my people were faring. Will the time never come when I can rule over England and unite my people? So many plans have I for their happiness and progress. Schools we must have. The Bible must be translated for the people to read. Roads must be built and the country made safe for all. How long must I sit in Cudred's cottage mending arrows when my heart wishes to help my suffering people!

Switha (*running in*). I thought I smelled them burning! Oh, thou lazy, useless fellow! Thou art ready enough to eat the cakes, but too lazy to keep them from burning. No wonder thou hast no home, idle as thou art.

Alfred. I pray thee, good dame, forgive me. I was lost in thought of happier days and forgot my duty. Really I am sorry.

Switha. Ay, ay, that is always the way with thee. That smooth tongue of thine is better to thee than silver or gold; for it obtains for thee food, lodging, and friends, and softens all the wrath thy faults provoke. However, I shall set by all the burnt cakes for thy portion of the week's bread, I promise thee; and thou shalt have no other till they are all eaten.

Alfred. My good mistress, here comes a pilgrim boy to ask thy charity. May I bestow one of these cakes on him?

Switha. Thou mayest do what thou wilt with thine own, man! but do not presume to give away my property to idle fellows like thyself.

Alfred. But, mistress, may I not give him that which was to have been my portion for dinner?

Switha. No, indeed! I have enough to do with feeding one vagrant without adding all the lazy pilgrims who pass by.

Alfred. See, mistress, my amulet! I will give thee this jewel, Switha, if thou wilt permit me to feed this poor pilgrim.

Switha. Very well, then. Give him thy portion while I go and hide the jewel.

[*Goes out as Odulph enters.*]

Alfred. Welcome, Odulph! Tell me thy tidings. I hunger for good news.

Odulph. My tidings, royal Alfred, are these: Hubba, the Dane, the terror of England, is slain, and his banner of the Raven waves in my father's hall!

Alfred. What? Is thy father's castle in the possession of the Danes?

Odulph. Not so, my royal master; but the banner of the Danes, captured by your victorious Saxons, hangs in his hall. We were pent up in the castle by the Danes till our provisions failed. When the last loaf was eaten, and our archers had launched their last arrows, my valiant father led the garrison in an attack upon the foe.

Alfred. Brave Oscar! And you defeated them!

Odulph. Yes, because of the carelessness of the Danes. They believed they had us in their power, and they never dreamed we would leave the castle walls. Few as we were, we fell upon them and slew their chiefs. The soldiers fled, and left our men victorious. Then my father raised the cry, "Alfred the king!" All the country is calling, "Alfred the king!"

Alfred. The time is ripe. I thank you, Odulph. Your father is a noble man, and I shall know how to show a king's gratitude to you both. Shall we go?

Odulph. Lead on, King Alfred, England is ready. Soon you shall head your army shouting, "Long live King Alfred!"

ROBIN HOOD AND THE SAD KNIGHT

PERSONS IN THE PLAY—Robin Hood, Little John, Midge, Will Scarlet, The Abbot, The Knight, The Prior, The Lord Chief Justice, The Lady

Scene I.—*In the Greenwood.*

[*Robin Hood and his men making arrows.*]

Robin Hood. This feather is too short. Give me another, Little John. This is a better one.

Midge. Making arrows is not a simple thing, is it, my master?

Robin Hood. Indeed, no; if the feathers be too short, the arrows will not keep true to their course; and if the feathers be too long, the arrows will not fly swiftly.

Little John. If all men knew how to make arrows, their skill in shooting would seem greater. Look to your arrows, say I, before you shoot.

Will Scarlet. We should thank the gray goose for the even growth of her feathers, which carries our arrows straight to the mark.

Robin Hood. First the strong bow that bends to our hand, then the straight arrow, tough and trim, and the feathers that wing it to its mark. But best of all the steady hand and keen eye that direct our winged shaft. But you have worked well this morning, my men, and now we may rest awhile. Sing us a song, Will Scarlet, while we lie beneath the friendly oak.

Will Scarlet (*sings*).

The hunt is up! the hunt is up!
  And it is well-nigh day;
And Harry our king has gone hunting
  To bring his deer to bay.

The east is bright with morning light,
  And darkness, it is fled;
And the merry horn wakes up the morn
  To leave his idle bed.

Awake, all men! I say again
  Be merry as you may!
For Harry our king is gone hunting
  To bring the deer to bay.

Little John. This song is well enough in its way, but for me, I should much prefer a good dinner. The morning's work has given me a fine appetite and I long for food.

Robin Hood. It is good to eat, but not before we find some rich traveler to pay the bill. Ride out, my man, and find us a host. Willing or unwilling, bid him come.

Little John. With right good will, my master; and may I soon meet with him!

Robin Hood. Remember well, no farmer shall you bring. He works for what he gets and shall live in peace. And the laborer who toils for wife and child you must not harm. Only those who oppress the poor and weak, those who are selfish and unkind, who play while others weep, these shall you bring to me.

Will Scarlet. But look, my master, what sorrowing knight rides there? His garments are rich and his horse gayly decked, but his countenance is sad and he rides slowly, careless of the way.

Little John. Hail, gentle knight; my master awaits you and fain would have your company at dinner.

The Knight. At dinner,—in the wood! Who is your master?

Little John. Robin Hood is he: and here he is to bid you welcome.

Robin Hood. Welcome, Sir Knight, thrice welcome art thou, for I have fasted beyond the dinner hour. Pray you, dismount.

The Knight. God save you and all your company!

Midge. The dinner is served, my master.

Robin Hood. Will you join us, Sir Knight? Here are pheasants and swans and meat of the deer.

The Knight. Such a good dinner, with so many brave men, I have not eaten for many a day. If I come again to this country, I will make thee as good a dinner. But Heaven knows when that will be!

Robin Hood. Thanks for your kind offer. But in the greenwood our guests must pay for their food. A yeoman does not pay for a rich knight!

The Knight. Sorry am I that you must call me poor. I would that I could pay you, but in my saddlebags are no more than ten shillings.

Robin Hood. Is that indeed the truth, Sir Knight? Look carefully, Little John; if the knight speaks truly, he shall keep the ten shillings, but if not—

Little John. Indeed, my master, the knight speaks truly, for this is all the money I can find.

Robin Hood. How comes it, noble knight, that thou art so poor? Come, tell me the story. Mayhap I can help thee.

The Knight. I am Sir Richard of Lea, and my ancestors have been knights for a hundred years. A year ago I had plenty of money to spend as I would. But now I have nothing for my wife and my children, who weep for my absence from them.

Robin Hood. But how did you lose all your money?

The Knight. Perhaps you will think I lost it in a foolish way. My son, whom I dearly love, is a manly youth. Well can he shoot and joust fairly in the field. But once, in a quarrel, he slew a youth, and to save him, I pledged all my lands. Unless I redeem them by All Saints Day I shall lose them all.

Robin Hood. What is the sum you are bound to pay?

The Knight. Four hundred pounds. The day is near and I have nothing.

Robin Hood. But what canst thou do if thou losest thy land? What wilt thou do?

The Knight. I will sail far away over the seas. I cannot remain in England.

Robin Hood. It is a small sum. Hast thou no friends to help thee in thy need?

The Knight. Many friends had I when I had money and lands. Now when I need their help they turn away and know me not.

Robin Hood. By my faith, gentle knight, thou shalt not want for a friend. Little John, go to the chest and count out four hundred pounds.

Will Scarlet. Shall he not have cloth for a coat, gentle master? He is thinly clad.

Robin Hood. Well said, Will Scarlet; go, get three measures of every kind, that he may be warmly and gayly clad.

Little John. Here is the money, Robin Hood, and good measure.

Robin Hood. And what will you give, Little John, who are so generous with my money?

Little John. A pair of golden spurs, that he may ride fast to his castle and redeem his lands.

The Knight. Many thanks, Little John, and to you, my good friend. Tell me, Robin Hood, when shall I come to return the money you so kindly lend me?

Robin Hood. This day twelvemonth; and a happy year may it be! We will meet under this trysting tree. Till then, be merry!

The Knight. I shall be with you a year from to-day. Farewell.

Scene II.—*In the Abbot's Hall*

The Abbot, The Prior

The Abbot. This day a year ago Sir Richard Lea borrowed four hundred pounds from me. He promised to pay in a year or lose his land. If he does not return to-day, the land will be mine.

The Prior. The day is now far spent. Perhaps he will come yet.

The Abbot. I am sure I hope he will not. I trust he has left England.

The Prior. The land is worth much more than four hundred pounds. It were a pity if he did not redeem it.

The Abbot. Thou art ever crossing me! Speak no more about it! Where is the Lord Justice?

Lord Justice (*enters*). Here I am. I have just come from London to do justice on that Knight. Where is he?

The Abbot. The Knight has failed to come with the money and this is the day when the land falls to me.

Lord Justice. I dare swear he will not come and thou shalt have his lands. I now declare that the knight, Sir Richard Lea, has failed to keep his promise and his lands are—

The Knight (*entering and kneeling before the Abbot*). Rejoice with me, Sir Abbot. I am come to keep my day.

The Abbot. What dost thou say? Hast brought the money?

The Knight (*to try the Abbot*). Not a penny, but—

The Abbot. What dost thou here without the money?

The Knight. To ask your kindness and patience, Sir Abbot, for a longer time.

Lord Justice. The day has come. Thou losest thy land, Sir Knight, since thou canst not pay.

The Knight. Good Lord Justice, help me against my foes! I will surely pay, but must have more time.

Lord Justice. I am sorry for thee, Sir Richard, but the law is plain. Either pay your debt or lose your land.

The Knight. Sir Abbot, I pray thee, have pity.

The Abbot. Get the land when thou canst, thou gettest no pity from me.

The Knight. By my faith, then, if I get not my land again, thou shalt pay dearly for it.

The Abbot. Get thee gone, false knight! Darest thou threaten me?

The Knight. False knight I am not, for I have fought well for my king.

Lord Justice. Sir Abbot, the day is not yet gone. What wilt thou give the knight to hold his peace?

The Abbot. A hundred pounds.

Lord Justice. Make it two hundred.

The Knight. No, nor nine hundred. Ye shall not have my land! Here, Sir Abbot, are the four hundred pounds. Had you been less covetous, I would have given interest. Now, get you gone, all of you; and learn to deal more justly and kindly with those in need. [*They go out.*]

Lady Lea (*entering*). Oh, my dear husband! how glad I am to hear your voice again.

The Knight. Happy am I to see you and to be at home again. I must tell you how kind Robin Hood has been to me.

Lady Lea. Robin Hood your friend? Is he not the outlaw of the forest?

The Knight. Yes; but he is kind to all who are unhappy or oppressed. He saved me from leaving England and gave me money to redeem my land.

Lady Lea. How I long to thank him for his goodness to you.

The Knight. In a year we will go to him and repay the four hundred pounds.

Lady Lea. I shall be glad to see him and his merry men, and try to thank them all.

WILLIAM TELL

A STORY OF SWITZERLAND. A.D. 1307

PERSONS IN THE PLAY—WILLIAM TELL; LEWIS, HIS SON; ALBERT, HIS SON; ANNETTE, HIS WIFE; LALOTTE, HIS NIECE, GESSLER, SOLDIERS

SCENE I.—*At Tell's Home*

Albert. Lewis, doesn't the quail smell good?

Lewis. Yes, I wish I could have some of it!

Lalotte. Hush! the quail is for your father.

Albert. I know that, Lalotte; but I am hungry, and I like quail.

Lalotte. Your father will be cold and hungry, for he has been on a long journey.

Albert. But perhaps he will not come. Mother, mother! may we have the quail if father is late? It is done now, and it will not be good if it is cooked any more.

Lalotte. Hush, you greedy boy! If I were your mother, I would send you to bed for thinking of such a thing.

Albert. You are not the mistress. You are not the mistress, and I shall not go to bed because you say so!

William Tell (at door). But you shall go to bed, young man, if your Cousin Lalotte tells you to do so. Take them to bed, Lalotte.

Albert. Oh, father! We were only joking.

Lewis. Please, father, don't send us to bed.

William Tell. I must, my boy, because it is late, and I have news for your mother. Good night, my sons.

Boys. Good night, dear father.

[*They go out with Lalotte.*]

William Tell. Thy father's news is not for young ears.

Annette. There is a sadness in thy voice, and trouble in thy face! Tell me what has happened to thee! Wilt thou not trust me?

79

William Tell. Yes, my Annette! Thou hast ever been a good wife and faithful friend. Why should I conceal my deeds from thee?

Annette. What hast thou done, my husband?

William Tell. Perhaps thou wilt blame me.

Annette. Nay, for thou art a good man, and whatever thou doest is right in my eyes.

William Tell. Thou knowest how our foreign rulers oppress the good people of Switzerland?

Annette. I do, but why should we poor peasants worry over the affairs of the nobles?

William Tell. But they are our troubles, too. So to-night I have met with three and thirty men, brave and loyal hearts, who have sworn to resist our oppressors and free our land from tyranny.

Annette. But how can three-and-thirty men think to conquer the armies of foreign tyrants?

William Tell. Sometimes great events are brought about by small means. All the people in their hearts hate the false ruler of our poor country, and many of these will willingly die for her sake.

Annette. Thou art brave, my husband, but what can so few do?

William Tell. Think of it! The father of one of our band has just been put to a cruel death. No man knows where the tyrant will strike next. Perhaps Gessler will pick me out for the next victim.

Annette. Thee! What charge could he bring against thee?

William Tell. He could say that I am the friend of my country, which in the tyrant Gessler's mind is a crime.

Annette. But Gessler will never hear of us, humble peasants. He is too far above us to care what we think.

William Tell. Not so, my dear wife. Gessler will not permit us to hold our thoughts in secret. He has a plan to discover our inmost thoughts.

Annette. What plan can he make to read our minds?

William Tell. A clever plan to tell a freeman from a slave. In Altdorf, our capital city, he has set up a pole. Upon the top of this pole he has put the cap of the Austrian king and has ordered every man to take off his hat as he passes by, to show that he yields to the Austrian rule. Is not this a brave plan? He who obeys the tyrant is a slave. Wouldst thou have thy husband doff his cap to his country's tyrant?

Annette. Never! I should despise thee, couldst thou do it!

William Tell. That is my own brave wife! Thou speakest as a free woman, the mother of free children, should speak. And our children shall be free! When I go to Altdorf I shall refuse to obey the order of Gessler and all Switzerland shall know that William Tell will not bow to a foreign tyrant.

Annette. But why go to Altdorf, my husband? Thou knowest the power of Gessler and his cruelty!

William Tell. Wouldst have me a coward? No, dear wife. When my business calls me to Altdorf I shall go and in all ways act as a free man, loyal to my country and afraid of no one.

Annette. Thou art a brave man, my husband, and I honor thee.

Scene II.—*Altdorf: The Market place*

William Tell, Albert, Soldiers, Gessler

William Tell. Come, my son, I have sold the chamois skins, and now I must buy the things your mother wished me to get for her.

Albert. And, father, please buy some toys for little Lewis.

William Tell. You are a good boy, Albert, to remember your little brother. We will go to the shop across the square and look there for toys.

Soldier. Halt, man! Salute yonder cap!

William Tell. Why should I salute a cap of cloth?

Soldier. It is the cap of our emperor. If you do not honor the cap, you are a traitor.

William Tell. I am no traitor, and yet I will not bow down to an empty cap. I am a true Swiss and love my country.

Gessler. Ha, ha! Then we have a traitor here who will not yield to our emperor! Arrest him, my men; and we will teach him his manners. Who is this man?

Soldier. His name is William Tell, my lord.

Gessler. Insolent traitor! Bind him well.

Albert. Oh, father, I am afraid. Do not let the soldiers take me.

William Tell. Be calm, my son. No harm will come to thee.

Gessler. Indeed, and is this your son? Has he come to mock the cap of our royal master, too? Seize the boy and bind him to yonder tree.

William Tell. What will you do with the boy? Does a captain war with a child?

Gessler. We shall see. I hear you are a famous shot, William Tell, and handle well the bow and arrow. We shall soon know your skill. Have you a good arrow in your quiver? Perhaps you can shoot an apple from the head of your child.

Soldier. Where shall I bind the boy, my captain?

Gessler. To yonder tree. If his father shoots the apple from his child's head, he shall go free. If he fails he must die. Are you ready?

William Tell. Rather would I die than risk killing my eldest son. Let him go, and take my life.

Gessler. That I shall not do. You must both die unless you save your lives as I have said. Will you try the shot or are you afraid?

William Tell. Bind the boy's eyes, I beg. He might move if he saw the arrow coming, and my skill would be in vain.

82

Gessler. I am willing, for well I know you cannot cleave the apple at that distance.

William Tell. Tyrant! I cannot fail now, when my son's life depends upon me. Stand perfectly still, my brave boy, and father will not hurt you. Now I pray for strength—my trusty arrow must not fail me! There! [*He shoots.*]

Soldier. See, my captain! The apple is split! That was a fine shot!

Gessler. Yes, it was a good shot, and I did not believe anyone could make it. I suppose I must set you free. But why have you that other arrow in your hand?

William Tell. To shoot you with it had I killed my darling boy.

Gessler. Seize him, my men!

William Tell. Never! Come, Albert! This arrow for him who stops me!

Soldiers. He has escaped!

TIME AND THE SEASONS

Father Time. I must call my children together and give them orders for the New Year. Open the door, my servants, and let the Seasons appear.

Spring (entering). Here I am, Father Time. What are your commands for your youngest daughter?

Father Time. Welcome, my dainty Spring! It is your duty to call the gentle rains to fall upon the thirsting ground. Yours is the pleasant task to paint the blades of young grass a delicate green. You call the birds back from the south and rouse all nature from her winter sleep. The winds blow freshly over the earth; the clouds move here and there, bringing the rain; and the bulbs, hidden under the soil, slowly push their leaves into the sunlight. What flowers will you bring to deck the earth?

Time and the Seasons

Spring. O Father Time! Look here upon my pretty flowers! Here is the snowdrop, so white and brave. It pushes its head up through the snow, which is no whiter than its own petals. And here I have a bunch of crocuses, blue, yellow, white, and of many colors. Aren't they pretty amid the grass? Then the gorgeous tulips, holding their heads so high, making the earth brilliant with their gay, bright colors. I think the golden daffodils and sweet narcissus are my favorite flowers, though I am very fond of what the children call spring beauty.

Father Time. I see, my daughter, that you love all your flower children, and that is right. All are beautiful, each in its own way. And now tell me what joys do you bring to the little children of the earth?

Spring. All the children love me. They hunt for the first flowers, they welcome the first birds returning from the south, and they prepare the garden for the seeds of flowers and vegetables. The boys play marbles everywhere, and run and laugh, filling their lungs with my life-giving air. The organ grinder plays for the children and they dance on the sidewalks, singing and calling out in delight. The trees put forth their tender leaves. The sun fills the air with golden warmth, and the world seems full of promise.

Father Time. Well done, my daughter. And now, my daughter Summer, tell me your plans for the year.

Summer. Dear father, I delay my coming until Spring has prepared the way. The air must be soft and warm to please me, and the earth must be prepared by the rains and the warm rays of the sun. The colors of my flowers are deeper and richer than those of sister Spring. I bring the lilies, the peonies, and the poppies. Best of all, the glowing roses open at my call, and fill the air with perfume.

Father Time. And the children, my fair daughter, what do you bring to them?

Summer. The dear children! I think they all like my sunny days and the long time for play. For July and August in many countries are given to the school children for their play time. Then they go to the seashore and play in the water and the sand; or to the country, where the green grass, the farmyard animals, and all the country games delight them.

Father Time. Children are so fond of play and the long summer days out-of-doors that I wonder what they think of you, my older daughter, Autumn?

Autumn. Children do like to play and I am glad they get so well and strong with the vacation my sister, Summer, gives them. Yet all children like to learn, too. We must not forget that. What joy it is to read the beautiful stories that great men and women have written for them. What delight they have in learning to write, to sing, to draw, and to make pretty objects of paper, clay, and wood.

Father Time. Yes, that is true, but have you no pleasures out-of-doors for them?

Autumn. Some people say my days are the most pleasant of the year. The gardens have many beautiful flowers, and the fruits are ripening in the orchards and vineyards. The apples hang red on the boughs, and children like to pick them and eat them, too! I have the harvest moon, the time when the farmers bring home the crops ripened by August suns, and the earth seems to gather the results of the year's work, the riches of field, orchard, and meadow. The squirrels gather their hoard of nuts and hide them away for their winter's food. Gay voices of nutting parties are heard in the woods, and all the air is filled with songs of praise and thanksgiving for the bounty of the year.

Father Time. Your work is surely one of worth and I rejoice with you, my daughter, in your happiness. You are a true friend of men, showing them that honest effort and its work will always bring proper reward. Now, my merry laughing child, what have you to tell us?

Winter. Some people think I am your oldest daughter, Father Time, but they forget that two of my months are always in the New Year. Although my hair and garments are white, the cold is only outside; my heart is warm. Have I not jolly St. Nicholas who never grows old? I cover the earth with my warmest blanket of softest snow, softer and whiter than ermine, and all the tender flowers sleep cozily and warm until sweet Spring awakes them. The children get out their sleds and skates, and the merry sleigh bells ring. What fun it is to build the snow man, and even if the hands get cold, the eyes shine brighter than in warm days and the cheeks are rosy as the reddest flower. "Hurrah for Winter!" shout the boys. The merriest holidays I have when all hearts are gay and filled with loving care for others. I would not change, dear Father Time, with any of my sisters. I say good-by to the passing year and welcome the new year. If the old year has had troubles and sorrows, all the people turn with hope to the new, and call to one another the wish, "A Happy New Year to all!"

Father Time. I am glad you are contented with the work you have to do. And now, my daughters, I must send you out upon your travels all over the world. May your coming bring peace; joy, and prosperity to all mankind!

THE GINGERBREAD MAN

PERSONS IN THE PLAY—THE LITTLE OLD WOMAN, THE GINGERBREAD MAN, THE BOY, THE FOX, CHILDREN, MEN, THE FARMER

SCENE.—*Home of Little Old Woman*

Little Old Woman. Now all my housework is done I think I will make some gingerbread. There is nothing quite so good for lunch as warm gingerbread and a glass of milk, or a cup of hot tea. I can make pretty good gingerbread, too, all of my friends say. Here is the flour and butter and molasses and milk. Now it is all ready to put into the pan. But I made too much this time. What shall I do with it? Nothing must be wasted in a good cook's kitchen. Oh, I know! I'll make a cunning gingerbread man for the little boy who lives next door.

Where is my knife? Now roll the dough very thin, cut out the round little head, then the neck, now the two arms, now the little fat body, and last the legs with high heels on the shoes. Well, this certainly is a fine little gingerbread man. I think I'll make a little hat with a wide brim. Now I'll put two currants for his eyes, two for his nose, three for his cute little mouth, and six for the buttons on his coat.

Then I'll sprinkle sugar and cinnamon over him and put him in the oven to bake.

Let me look at the clock. It is half past eleven. At twelve the gingerbread man will be baked, ready for the little boy when he comes home from school.

Well, I've washed the dishes, and set the table for my lunch, and it is now just twelve o'clock. I'll open the oven door and see if my gingerbread man is ready.

Oh! what was that! Why, it is the gingerbread man!

Gingerbread Man. Yes, it is the gingerbread man, and now I'll go and see the world.

Little Old Woman. Go! you mustn't go! You belong to me.

Gingerbread Man.

Ah, ha! ah, ha! catch me, if you can!
You can't catch me, I'm a gingerbread man!

Little Old Woman. There he goes, out of the door, just as if he were really a little boy, and not made of something good to eat! Come back; come back!

Gingerbread Man.

> Ah, ha! ah, ha! catch me, if you can!
> You can't catch me, I'm a gingerbread man!

Little Old Woman. I know I can't run as fast as he can. There he goes out of the gate. There are some men who are working in the street. I'll ask them to catch him. Help! help me catch the gingerbread man!

Men. Yes, ma'am. Where is he? Oh, there he is, the little rascal! We'll catch him.

Gingerbread Man.

> Ah, ha! ah, ha! catch me, if you can!
> You can't catch me, I'm a gingerbread man!

Men. Well, there he goes and he does run fast! Come, let us run after him!

Little Old Woman. Oh, I know the men can't run as fast as he can, and they will never catch my gingerbread man! Here are the children coming from school. I'll call them. Children, children!

Children. Yes, little old woman, here we are. What did you call us for?

Little Old Woman. Oh, my dear children, see the gingerbread man I made for the little boy next door! There he goes running as fast as he can, and I can't catch him!

Boy. And the men are running after him, and they can't catch him either. Just watch me, little woman, I'll catch him for you.

Gingerbread Man.

> Ah, ha! ah, ha! catch me, if you can!
> You can't catch me, I'm a gingerbread man.

Girl. I have my roller skates on. Perhaps I can catch him!

Little Old Woman. I'm sure you can, my child.

Girl. I'll try. Look out, Mr. Gingerbread Man!

Gingerbread Man.

> Ah, ha! ah, ha! catch me, if you can!
> You can't catch me, I'm a gingerbread man!

Little Old Woman. There he goes, and none of them can catch him. Now he is near some farmers. I'll call on them to help me. Farmer, farmer, will you please help me catch the gingerbread man? There he goes over your wheat field.

Farmer. Yes, indeed, we'll help you. Here, you gingerbread man, keep out of my wheat field! Come, men; run after him and catch him.

Men. We'll catch him before he gets to the fence.

Gingerbread Man.

> Ah, ha! ah, ah! catch me, if you can!
> You can't catch me, I'm a gingerbread man!

Little Old Woman. Oh, dear! Oh, dear! there he goes into the wood, and no one can run fast enough to catch him.

Farmer. I'm sorry, madam, but we must go back to our work on the farm.

Boy. Hark! listen! don't you hear the little gingerbread man calling?

Gingerbread Man.

> Ah, ha! ah, ha! catch me, if you can!
> You can't catch me, I'm the gingerbread man!

Little Old Woman. Yes, he is calling to us from the wood. I thank you, children, and now we will go home.

Gingerbread Man (*in the wood*). Ah, ha! and they didn't catch me! and now I am free to play in the wood. What a pleasant place!

Mr. Fox. Well, what sort of a funny little man is this?

Gingerbread Man.

Ah, ha! ah, ha! catch me, if you can!
You can't catch me, I'm a gingerbread man!

Mr. Fox. Can't I? Well, I *have* caught you; and now let me see if you are good to eat. First, I'll try one of your arms. That tastes good!

Gingerbread Man. I'm going!

Mr. Fox. And now the other arm!

Gingerbread Man. I'm going!

Mr. Fox. Now for the leg.

Gingerbread Man. I'm going!

Mr. Fox. Really, Mr. Gingerbread Man, I think you are very good eating for a hungry fox. Now I'll taste the other leg.

Gingerbread Man. I'm going!

Mr. Fox. Now for your round little body.

Gingerbread Man. I'm going!

Mr. Fox. There is not very much left. Just your head for the last mouthful.

Gingerbread Man. I'm gone!

Mr. Fox. Yes, you're gone; and a very nice meal, Mr. Gingerbread Man.

THE GOOD FAIRY

Scene I.—*In the Wood*

The Good Fairy. At last I am in this wood where I must save the Lady Alice from danger. How dark it seems here after the bright light of my skyey home. Surely I shall be glad to return to the courts of fairyland. Yet it is pleasant to be of service to the young and innocent, to those who are good and true. Some there are on earth who do not love the truth, who do not do the things that are honest and kind, and they must be punished. Kind and gentle deeds must be rewarded with our help.

Here in this dark grove dwells Comus, an evil spirit, who loves not the good. Here he finds the unlucky traveler and takes him to his court. There he offers him food and a pleasant drink. But in the glass is a potion which drives memory from the mind and makes one forget home and friends. Then the unhappy traveler loses his human head and must have the head of some animal or bird. Comus enjoys seeing his victims act like wild and foolish animals or the forest.

In this dangerous wood the Lady Alice and her brothers are wandering, and my duty it is to protect them from the evil Comus. Hark! I think I hear the noisy band. Here will I hide and listen.

[*Comus and his crew enter; men and women with animal heads.*]

Comus. Now the sun has gone from the western heavens and the star of night shines over us. This is the hour we love the best. All the serious, wise old people who love the day and its work are weary now and have gone to bed. We who love fun and a merry dance, we wake when the sky is flecked with golden stars. Now the moon calls the fairies from brook and fountain to play their merry games and sing. These are the joys of night in our dark and secret grove. Come, make a merry ring and dance. No care have we nor fear. We will dance and sing until the first ray of light is seen in the east.

[*They dance until Comus speaks.*]

Comus. Break off! break off! I hear a footstep not our own approaching this place. Run to your places lest you frighten the traveler whoever it may be.

[*They disappear.*]

I believe some maiden approaches. I will weave my spells and appear to her in the dress of a shepherd and she will not be afraid. Here she comes. I will step aside and learn how she happens to be alone in my grove.

[Comus hides.]

Lady Alice (entering). I thought I heard the sound of noisy merrymaking,— with music as if many were dancing. Here was the sound, but here I see no one. Alas! I should be sorry to meet rude youths, but where can I go, what can I do, left alone in this dark and gloomy wood? O my brothers, where are you? When they saw me wearied, unable to go farther, they left to find me nourishment and shelter, promising soon to return. Truly they must be lost in this vast forest. O dark night, why have you stolen the way from them and left me alone and helpless? Helpless? No, not helpless, for the good mind has helpers ever present in pure-eyed Faith and white-handed Hope. I will pray to God, who will send me a guardian to guide me to my home. What is that light I see? My brothers seek me and I will sing to them. Perhaps they are not far away and will hear my voice.

> Sweet Echo, sweetest nymph, that liv'st unseen
> > Within thy airy shell,
> Canst thou not tell me of a gentle pair
> > That likest thy Narcissus are?
> O if thou have
> > Hid them in some flowery cave,
> Tell me but where,
> Sweet Queen of Parley, Daughter of the Sphere!

Comus (to himself). What sweet song is this? Can any mortal sing with such charm and beauty? Such sacred and home-felt delight I never heard till now. I'll speak to her, and she shall be my queen.

Comus (dressed as a shepherd). Hail, fair goddess! for you must be more than mortal, to sing such sweet and wondrous strain.

Lady Alice. Nay, gentle shepherd. I sang not as loving my own voice, and praise is lost that falls on unattending ears. Stern necessity compelled my song.

Comus. How comes it, Lady, that you are thus alone?

Lady Alice. My brothers left me upon a grassy turf. Darkness came upon the grove, and I fear they are lost.

Comus. Were they men full grown or still young?

Lady Alice. Young and fair my brothers are.

Comus. Two such I saw, so lovely in their youthful grace I thought I looked upon some fairy scene. If these are the lads you seek, we can easily find them.

Lady Alice. Gentle villager, quickly tell me the shortest way to them!

Comus. Due west it lies.

Lady Alice. To find it out, good shepherd, would be too difficult in this darkness to a stranger.

Comus. I know every step, fair lady, for I live close by and daily tread the path in caring for my sheep. Gladly will I conduct you and find your brothers if they are still in this grove. Till daybreak you can rest in a cottage near by, where you will be safe until you wish to travel on.

Lady Alice. Kind shepherd, I take your word, and gladly go to the shelter you mention. Kindness is often found in lowly homes. Lead on, and I will follow.

Comus. This way, fair lady!

SCENE II.—*Another Place in the Forest*

Elder Brother. How our steps are stayed by the darkness of the night and of the forest. Would that the moon and stars would pierce the clouds! If only we could see some faint glimmer of a candle in some lowly hut that would guide us on our way.

Second Brother. Or hear the folded flocks, or sound of village flute or song, or if the cock would crow the watches of the night! Where can our dear sister be now? Does she wander in the deep grove, or against the rugged bark of some broad elm lean her head in fear? Perhaps even while we speak she is the prey of some savage beast!

Elder Brother. Cease, brother, to dream of evils that may not be. No good can come from false alarms. I do not believe my good sister has lost herself in fear. Her faith will keep her calm.

Second Brother. I do not fear the darkness and the fact that she is alone. But I do fear some harm may come to her from rude wanderers in the wood.

Elder Brother. Yet I believe she is so good and true that evil has no power to harm her. All powers of good surround her and drive evil away. But list! Some faint call sounds on my ear.

Second Brother. Yes, I hear it now. What should it be?

Elder Brother. Either some one lost in this wood, like ourselves, or else some roving woodman, or perhaps some robber calling to his fellows!

Second Brother. God save my sister!

Elder Brother. Who comes here? Speak! Advance no further!

Spirit (as a shepherd). What voice is that? Speak once again.

Second Brother. O brother! 'tis my father's shepherd, sure.

Elder Brother. Are you Thyrsis? How could you find this dark, secluded spot? Why did you come?

Spirit. To find out you. But where is your lovely sister? Why is she not with you?

Elder Brother. Without our fault we lost her as we came.

Spirit. Alas, then my fears are true!

Elder Brother. What fears, good Thyrsis?

Spirit. I have long known that this wood was held in the power of an evil spirit, and this evening as I sat me down upon a bank I heard most lovely

94

strains as if an angel sang. Listening, I knew it was your sister's voice. I hastened to her and heard her tell Comus of you whom she had lost. To you I came that we may save her from the evil spirit of the wood.

Elder Brother. Let us hasten to attack him with our swords.

Spirit. Alas! Your bravery I praise, but it is vain. The evil charm of Comus can be broken only by a wondrous plant. See, I have it here. With this will we overcome his fairy spells.

Elder Brother. Thyrsis, lead on! And some good angel bear a shield before us!

SCENE III.—*The Palace of Comus*

Comus. Drink, Lady, of the wine. You are faint and weary, and this will refresh you. Do not refuse!

Lady Alice. Never will I drink the potion in that glass. You may control the body, but my free mind you can never bind.

Comus. Why are you angry, Lady? Here is a place filled with all delight.

Lady Alice. Is this the cottage you told me of, the place of safety where I could rest. None but good men can offer good things. I will never drink what you offer. What monsters are these? I pray Heaven guard me!

Comus. Dear Lady, stay with me and be my queen. Here may you reign over all my kingdom. See what royal robes are mine, what jewels, what costly tables and shining gold and silver. No sorrow shall you know, but only joy and pleasure.

Lady Alice. Cease your words. You cannot move the mind guided by honesty and truth. You cannot frighten me, for well I know goodness is stronger than evil, truth is more powerful than falsehood. The pure heart cannot be harmed.

Comus. Cease, cease! all this is foolishness. Be wise and taste. All trouble will be forgotten. Come, I insist!

[*The brothers rush in and drive Comus and his crew away. But Lady Alice is entranced and cannot move.*]

Spirit. Have you let him escape? You should have seized his wand. Without that he has no power, but now we must have help to release your sister from his wicked power. The goddess of our river Severn, the lovely Sabrina, has power over all the enchantments of Comus. Her will I call.

Sabrina fair,

> Listen, where thou art sitting,
> Goddess of the silver lake,
> Listen and save.

Come from your home in the coral caves of the sea and help this lovely maiden in distress.

Sabrina (*entering*).

> From off the waters fleet,
> Thus I set my printless feet
> O'er the cowslip's velvet head
> That bends not as I tread;
> Gentle swain, at thy request
> I am here!

Spirit. Dear goddess, we implore your powerful aid to undo the charm wrought by the enchanter on this maiden.

Sabrina. 'Tis my greatest joy to help the pure and good. Gentle Lady, look on me. Thrice upon thy finger tips, thrice upon thy lips, I sprinkle drops from my pure fountain. Then I touch this marble seat and break the spell. All is well. Farewell.

Spirit. Fair Sabrina, for this aid I pray that all the pretty rills will never cease to flow into your broad river. May your banks ever be fair with groves and meadows sweet, while all men shall praise you for your gentle deeds. Farewell. Now, Lady, let us hasten from this grove. Your parents await their dear children, and we must hasten ere they become alarmed over your delay. Thanks to your pure heart and the aid of the fair Sabrina, you have come safely through the enchanter's wood.

9 783752 374704